Escape on the Astral Express

Escape on the Astral Express

A Novel

Harald Lutz Bruckner

Escape on the Astral Express: A Novel

Copyright © 2019 Harald Lutz Bruckner. All rights reserved. No part of this book may be reproduced or retransmitted in any form or by any means without the written permission of the publisher.

Published by Hideaway Park Press
Green Valley, AZ

ISBN: 978-0-578-50659-3 (paperback)
ISBN: 978-0-578-50661-6 (ebook)
LCCN: 2019905965

This is a work of fiction. Names, characters, places and incidents either are the product of the author's imagination or are used fictitiously, and any resemblance to actual persons, living or dead, business establishments, events, or locales is entirely coincidental.

rev201901

Books by Harald Lutz Bruckner

The Blue Sapphire Amulet

The Birken Saga
A Trilogy

Book 1 *Escape on the Astral Express*
Book 2 *A Wanderer on the Earth*
Book 3 *The Born-Again Phoenix*

For Lynne and Heddy

1931–1939

Prologue

ON New Year's Day 1931, Helena Birken found herself on her hands and knees, scrubbing wooden floors. Beads of moisture covered her brow; for that matter, she was drenched in perspiration all over her body and beginning to feel she needed to call it quits for the day and take a refreshing bath.

"Phew, this is not exactly how I envisioned spending my honeymoon with Alex. I've never been spoiled; I've also never worked as hard in my life, cleaning up other people's dirt."

Finally it sunk in—this hotel wasn't "other people's" any longer. It belonged to her and her husband, Alex Birken; therefore it was their responsibility to give it new life. The tragedy was that they took over the business under decidedly upstream economic conditions.

Many believed the impact of the 1929 crash pushed European countries into a deeper abyss than the depression experienced in the United States. That certainly appeared to be true in Germany. Initially, the young couple's struggles had been eased by generous financial infusions from Helena's father. After all, it was he who pushed the marriage and taking over the hotel, but both Alex and Helena were inexperienced in running a business, never mind a large hotel.

X

On September 20, 1931, Helena's parents celebrated their twenty-fifth wedding anniversary. In preparation for the event, they arranged for the services of a professional photographer. Looking pretty for formal photographs was not exactly what Helena needed at the moment. But to appease her parents, she chose to make herself available. While she had every intention of joining her family for the anniversary celebration, attendance of the command performance with the photographer went against her grain. Reluctantly, she let Alex stay behind to manage the hotel in spite of never trusting him to do the job to her satisfaction.

Helena was glad her sister Elsa had fetched her at the train station; she wasn't sure she would have made it riding on the street-car. Sitting endlessly for the family portraits, her own life flashed in front of her eyes. She had recently celebrated her twenty-fourth birthday. Helena recalled the day in 1915 when her father left to do his military duty. She could still see all those gold coins piled on that huge table in the nook next to the store before her father cemented the filled cigar boxes into the basement chimney. A detailed map would later confirm the location of each hidden container.

Her sisters were staring at Helena, since she looked absolutely panic-stricken. Elsa heard Helena whisper in desperation.

"I wish that photographer would move a bit faster with changing those plates and get this show on the road. I don't know how long I can sit here looking smart and smiling. I feel like I have to heave again. Darn this pregnancy!"

Helena reached for her youngest sister's hand, conveying she didn't want to disrupt the photo session. Just studying her father's face, she knew her parents would be terribly upset if the photographer needed to be paid for additional time or, worse, would have to reschedule the photo session. The latter option was completely out of the question for Helena; one extra trip to Essen was more than enough. She closed her eyes for a moment, only to be admonished by the photographer.

"Please, everyone, stay with me and keep your eyes focused on me."

Helena made up her mind to daydream, forcing herself to keep her eyes wide open. She recalled the day when her father came home from the war. Helena loved holding her youngest sister, Georgine, when she was born in 1919. Helena left school a year later to spend a year in Davos, Switzerland, to receive treatment for her bout with tuberculosis. She remembered the many nights during the early 1920s of sitting in the nook with her mother; her brother, Arthur; and her sister Elsa, bundling all those gigantic bills of worthless money during the height of the inflation. Edged in her mind were the arguments with her father about pursuing studies at a university.

"Women don't belong in a university. They learn how to run a household, help their husbands in their business, and have children. I still don't believe they gave women the right to vote!" Her father was a classic male chauvinist.

Helena hated the first school of refinement to which she was sent. It turned out to be a school for scandal.

One of the happiest years, 1926, she spent in ancestral Swabia. While she learned many domestic skills, she also became acquainted with Hitler's *Mein Kampf*, published the year before. Helena abhorred the Nazis. She was disgusted with planned actions predicted by their future leader.

She recalled seeing Alex for the first time when he started working for her father in 1928. While she liked him very much, she wasn't so sure about the shotgun approach to their wedding. Her father had insisted on Alex and her marrying during Christmas 1930. She believed Friedrich Krämer was more interested in salvaging Alex's inherited hotel than his daughter's happiness.

The pop of the last flashbulb rocked Helena out of her reverie.

There was no use living in the past. She had to face the present. "Are we quite finished with taking photos? I need to use the loo. Excuse me. I'm about to vomit all over damnation." She rushed for the closest WC.

In 1932 she gave birth to her first son. Helena discovered that her small body was not designed for giving birth to large babies. Albert's birth weight exceeded five kilos. The delivery was long and painful; it almost took her life. She had worked until the last minute before Alex took her to the hospital. Like most expectant mothers in those days, Helena practiced what doctors advised—she always ate for two.

Feeling guilty about her unwelcome absence, her indomitable spirit caused her to be back in the mix of things in less than a week—a circumstance almost unheard of in Germany in 1932. Helena was fighting for her and her family's existence. She could deal with personal problems. Help was hired to take care of her firstborn. Of course, Gerda, the nursemaid, could take care of everything but breastfeeding the baby. No matter how hard Helena worked, she was helpless against the onslaught of creditors demanding payment for debts incurred by those who had mismanaged the property before she and Alex took over.

The year after Albert's birth, the Birkens made the acquaintance of two hotel guests, Alphons von Bickel and Lothar Zend. Alphons and Lothar became regulars on the premises. They always stayed at the hotel and shared a room. Alex bowled with the guys, but more importantly, it marked the beginning of an intellectual friendship between Helena and Alphons. They had discovered a shared love for the great writers of the German language. After closing the bar, they would nurse a nightcap and enjoy their privacy. They could freely exchange opinions about the political scene and on current authors like Thomas Mann and Bertolt Brecht. Both Alphons and Lothar would affect the Birken family in years to come.

Albert was almost two years old. There was no question that he was a beautiful child. When Albert sat in his fancy pram being taken for regular walks, people stopped to look at the boy with his crop of wavy blond hair. His smile and his bright blue eyes were infectious. Strangers would stop and ask if they could take photos. If the thought had ever crossed her mind, Helena could have made a fortune had she entered Albert into any sort of photo contest. He would have made a perfect poster boy. And, of course, he had conquered the hearts of his grandparents and all his uncles and aunts.

Helena gave it her all; she was savvy and learned to distinguish between excellent employees and those who didn't care. She quickly discovered how to learn from others and then use such information to her advantage. She made every effort to keep the slowly sinking ship afloat.

Helena Birken opposed, whenever possible, fascist intrusions into her business and daily life. On a Sunday morning in May 1933, she was checking the inventory in the hotel's bar. It was early, and she had already made sure the newspapers were available for the hotel and restaurant guests. In those days, it was customary to have all local and national newspapers hung on wooden sticks in foyers for the visiting public. But there was one she always ignored.

Two young Brownshirts ventured into the restaurant being full of self-importance. It was almost as if Helena had been lying in wait for them. After scanning the display, they clearly didn't realize who they were addressing.

"Ma'am, you don't have the *Nationalzeitung* on display," said one.

"Bah! That Nazi rag shall never hang in this establishment as long as I am the proprietor." She was ready to spit in the intruder's face.

"You will regret what you said," retorted the other young man, seeking to add menace, but his voice was somewhat squeaky and didn't sufficiently impress Helena.

She responded by giving them the hand signal for asshole, repeating it twice. They got the message; Helena made sure these men hadn't any doubt as to her opinion of members of the Nazi Party. The intruders left the Hotel Böcklin, cussing the owner of the establishment.

The following week, her husband was jumped by a bunch of Nazi hoodlums. He was walking home after an evening of bowling when six guys assaulted him. Although outnumbered, Alex Birken was a big man and in excellent shape. Three of his attackers wound up in a hospital. Alex just went home.

"What happened to you?" Helena asked as he walked into their apartment. "Who did this? Go straight to the bathroom. I need to treat those cuts on your face and hands."

"Apparently, those guys checking on the Nationalzeitung didn't appreciate being called assholes," he replied as he shrugged off his jacket. One sleeve was almost torn off.

"Well, I'm sorry for you, but I don't care what they thought of my gestures," she said as she pulled first-aid items from the cupboard under the sink. "That rag will never hang in the lobby here as long as we are the owners."

⋇

By 1934, Hitler had been in power for barely a year. Helena was riding in a cab with Alex, about to deliver her second child.

"What shall we name this child?" asked Helena on the way to the hospital. "How about Paula or Christine, after your mother?" Completely absentminded, Alex was already rolling his ball at the bowling tournament he was about to attend that night.

"Whatever you determine is fine with me. I know you are set on having a girl, but what if it is another boy?"

"You have any ideas?" posed Helena, looking at Alex with wide-open eyes.

"How about this one: We'll name him after the guy who garners the highest score on the bowling team tonight. I hope you don't object, but after I check you in at the hospital, I'm planning on joining Alphons, Lothar, and the team. As big as you are, you'll be in labor for a long time." Helena was dumbfounded.

"You must be joking about naming our child after a guy who gets the highest bowling score. Who ever heard of such an idea? I hope to God there isn't an Adolf on your team. God forbid! I'll assure you of one thing: were an Adolf to be the winner, no boy of mine will be named after him, although it has become one of the most popular names these days."

Helena was relieved to learn that it was Hektor Blumenstrauss who attained the highest score. She reluctantly agreed with Alex to bestow the winner's name on their second son.

Hektor's delivery required the use of forceps. His head appeared to be slightly lopsided, and his face had all sorts of markings. He definitely was not a poster child.

After she was discharged from the hospital, Helena was determined to get more help from Alex in managing the hotel. It seemed like all responsibilities were put on her shoulders. She believed that it was high time for Alex to do his part.

"Alex, you need to get more involved with the running of the hotel. I can't do it all alone. Also, I need to spend more time with our boys. You heard that Hektor's baptism needs to be postponed, didn't you? They locked up Pastor Domsdorf. He opened his mouth against the Nazis just once too often."

"Well, I'll try and help, but you know I never had much experience in running a hotel."

"Where do you think I got my training? I learned on the job, and you'd better get with it and do the same. Remember, this was your inheritance and not mine, although I have visions that a good share of my family's treasure has already been fettered away on this bottomless barrel." He could tell she was on the brink of crying, prompting Alex to take her in his arms and console her.

Helena sought joy and personal rewards in her thriving children. She'd often walk into the nursery, delighted to surprise her younger son.

"What are you doing, Hektor? Are you playing with your cute little toes?" Being not quite two years old, she would catch Hektor intensely listening to the music broadcast from the Apollo Theater, located across the street from the hotel.

"I see you like listening to Jan Kiepura and Marta Eggerth. You must be taking after your father." As soon as a recording with Jan Kiepura stopped playing, Hektor would speak clearly.

"Uncle, more." Helena didn't trust her ears.

Alex finally began to realize that not all was right in the fatherland. The euphoria resulting from the election promises that put Hitler into power three years earlier was quickly evaporating. Helena had never been blindsided by all this talk of a return to prosperity, national pride, and superiority after cleansing the nation of Jews and other undesirable persons. Helena's days were long, depriving her of much-needed sleep.

No matter how hard she tried, she could not stem the tide. In 1937 the Birkens went bankrupt, and the hotel was sold to the highest bidder.

Her father believed he had done everything to give his eldest daughter a good start in life and finally expressed his opinion. "Enough is enough!" They were told they had to fend for themselves; thus, Helena and her family moved back to Essen, the city of her birth. Helena was hurt and humbled, yet not totally defeated. She had inherited too much spunk from her father. Helena had tried and failed; it was time to move on.

On their first weekend back in town, Helena saw an ad in the morning paper. The job offer intrigued her. She made her first move by calling the owner, who was someone she'd known for years, a likable competitor of her father.

"Hallo, Herr Graf. Helena Krämer-Birken calling."

"How are you? Long time no see. What can I do for you?"

"I'm glad you recognized my name. I'm very much interested in the position you advertised in the paper. When may I speak with you in person?

"How about Monday morning? I'll meet you at the branch in Holsterhausen. I look forward to seeing you, Helena."

She wanted to be there an hour earlier and scope out the store. Helena needed to be prepared to snag the job from Herr Graf to make enough money and keep a roof over her family. She knew Alex could never do it. Helena stood unobtrusively among customers in the butcher shop when Herr Graf walked in. She approached him and shook his hand firmly.

"It's a very up-to-date property, Herr Graf. I could see myself running this place. The window displays could be a bit more exciting. Whoever is at the butcher block perhaps could do a better selling job. I can wield knives and cleavers and give quick references to recipes from my head at the same time. It often helps to sell a more challenging piece of meat." Herr Graf was astounded.

"Young lady, you just got yourself a job. It's all yours. Go for it."

Felix Graf wanted to check out Helena a month later. He had been impressed by the receipts since Helena had taken charge of the butchery. Felix chose to just walk in unannounced on a Saturday morning. The store was packed with shoppers. Helena was swinging away with a cleaver while giving cooking instructions to her customer on how to create a pocket on the calf's breast she was selling and recited the recipe for a delicious stuffing. She looked up and spotted her boss in the back of the line. She couldn't help reading approval on his face. A smile stole across hers. Helena was tempted to say something for which she might be sorry. She dismissed the idea immediately.

"I told you so!" was not what Herr Graf would have appreciated.

Helena had arrived, but again, her immediate family had to play second fiddle. She was not a neglectful parent; she simply took charge and knew where her priorities lay. Alex could take charge of Albert, but Hektor needed to be sent to a children's institution until the dust settled at home. By 1938 she had made enough money to surprise Alex.

"I want to open a meat market and grocery store of our own in Essen West. The business and apartments are in a brand-new building just finished on Kupferstrasse. It suits our needs, and the price is right. I met with the holding company this morning and signed a ten-year lease." Alex didn't know what to say. He felt totally outmaneuvered, useless, helpless, and outdone by his wife.

1939–1945

Chapter I

THE morning mail had been pushed through the mail shoot of the front door. The pile of letters smacked the tiled floor with an ear-catching noise. Alex gave a quick glance at various envelopes. His eyes struck one addressed to him; he slid it open with the large butcher knife he held in his hand.

"I've been called up for active duty. I need to report in Krefeld by the fifteenth of July. How will you handle the boys and the store? Don't you think you ought to give up this business and move into an apartment?"

"How the hell do you expect us to live? It wouldn't even be a measly sustenance on those few lousy Reichsmarks Herr Hitler is willing to pay you for your service to the glorious cause."

Just looking at her splotchy red face, Alex could tell Helena was in rare form. It didn't take much these days to get her fired up. She had become totally enraged by what she saw happening to her country. She was beginning to feel ashamed of being German. In her heart, it was the country of Goethe, Schiller, Kant, Bach, Beethoven, Brahms, and Frederick the Great, not a country controlled and run by a bunch of hoodlums who were seeking to exterminate some of her closest and dearest friends. Vehemently striking the butcher block with her handy cleaver, she was ready to give Alex his marching orders.

"When you get to the barracks in Krefeld, inform your leaders about your background. Being a master butcher, you might make a great cook. That way you won't have to be on the front lines when it comes to actual fighting. You never even liked butchering the animals. How can you even think of shooting another man or running a bayonet through him?"

He raised his fists in anger, disliking the things Helena was saying. And yet tears were running down his face. As always, she had spoken the truth. He wasn't a coward, but he had a hard time envisioning himself killing another human being. Helena's Jewish friends used to call him a real "Mensch." That expression said it all.

Helena drove him in her little Steyr to the *Hauptbahnhof*—the main railway station. Alex puckered his lips. It wasn't a lingering kiss she gave him; nevertheless, she kissed him goodbye. Sex was the last thing on her mind. Helena had too many other things worrying her—her parents, her boys, her close relatives, her friends, her neighbors, and the store. She was most concerned about the "great leader." He had shown his true markings, ruling the country with an iron fist and shouting about conquering the world from the day he gained control of Germany.

Helena had to stay involved. No way was she going to close the enterprise. She had made too many good friends at the markets she shopped every Monday through Friday morning. Getting up during early hours to help them had become part of her daily routine. For most transactions, Helena didn't need a calculator. She did it all in her head; she'd spit out correct totals before another even touched a mechanical aide. When needed, she could operate any typewriter or tabulator. Helena was proud of the fact that she was useful and that others appreciated her skills.

When she closed the store at six o'clock on Friday, September 1, 1939, she made up her mind that she had to see her family that night. Deep in her gut, she knew something terrible was about to happen. Unlike Georgine, she didn't believe in astrologers, ghosts, clairvoyance, crystal balls, tarot cards, or reading palm lines and tea leaves. She often had inner voices speaking to her and was inclined to listen to them. Helena usually found them to be correct.

"Boys, get your coats and caps. I am taking you to see Uncle Gottlieb and Aunt Marla. Grandpa and Grandma will be there, too, perhaps even Uncle Heinz and Uncle Wally." She slapped her latest acquisition—a rather flat rattan hat—on her head. Jokingly, she called it her *Bratpfanne* [frying pan].

"Are you ready, boys? *Kein Herumtrödeln* [no dilly-dallying] tonight. I can't drive the car, since visiting relatives doesn't qualify as a crucial business transaction. Lord knows what might happen if I were stopped by some Nazi. The streetcar it is. Let's go!" She held her large bundle of keys in her hand, ready to lock the front door. Helena was a great believer in locking everything, much to the dismay of others.

The trio walked the three blocks to the tram station. They arrived at the Reuters's house before six thirty. Hugs and kisses were exchanged, and they were ready to sit down at the dinner table. The men were congregating at one end, and the women and children sat at the other. Snippets of the word *Krieg* [war] could be overheard in the conversation among the men.

"Just look at this huge scar on my left temple. I was lucky the shrapnel wasn't any bigger or hit me any harder. I wouldn't be sitting with you at this table," said Uncle Gottlieb. "It's only twenty-one years since the Great War. How can any of us face another?"

The men stayed with their cigars and brandy, continuing their talk of war. Walter, or Uncle Wally, as the boys called him, had traveled by train from Marburg University. He was in the final throes of becoming a pediatrician. Because of his status as a future physician, he was excused from military duty at this time. Hitler needed doctors, any kind of medical doctors. His nineteen-year-old brother,

Heinz, was trained as a butcher. There were no excuses for him; he met Hitler's need for cannon fodder. He was called to serve and would leave within hours to join the military. Walter had come home to bid his younger brother farewell and console his parents. The Reuters shared a loving relationship with each other and their sons.

Not wanting to upset the young boys, Helena had them play with coloring books or other toys Aunt Marla had on hand. She, her mother, and her aunt were huddled in a corner on one of the large sofas. Waltraute knew that her only son, Arthur, would be among the first to be drafted and shipped off to wherever. Aunt Marla's eyes were red from crying all evening.

"Heinz is so young; he isn't even of legal age. How can they take him away from me?" Aunt Marla sputtered between sobs.

Shortly after nine o'clock, Helena collected her boys. Decked out with her *Bratpfanne* and her ever-ready umbrella, Helena was anxious to get home. Uncle Heinz picked up Hektor and gave him a firm hug.

"You be a good boy now; we all love you very much."

The Reuters were aware of Hektor's disastrous experiences when he was sent for extended periods to children's institutions far from home when he was just three years old, and again at age five.

Helena and her boys walked the darkened streets and caught their streetcar to the Hauptbahnhof. Their noses pressed to the dirty window, the boys got their mother's attention.

"*Mutti*, why are all those men in uniform standing around? There must be hundreds of them. What's going on?" Mother Birken turned toward the window, beholding the sea of uniformed men.

"I don't know. I'm as baffled as you are."

She normally knew what was happening; Helena was well informed, especially regarding matters involving the prevailing political scene. War had been imminent. Somehow, perhaps because of wishful thinking, she had not expected it to start so soon. She needed to get someone else's opinion to set things straight in her mind.

Mother Birken turned to the streetcar conductor as she and the boys were getting off.

"Do you have any idea why all these soldiers are here?"

"Ma'am, don't you know that Germany invaded Poland today? We are at war as we speak. These men in their infantry green are being sent east to complete the invasion. Is your husband in the army?"

"Yes, he was drafted six weeks ago. He was stationed in a barracks just outside Krefeld."

"He's probably been through here earlier on his way east."

"Do you think Papa is among these men?" asked the boys.

"I don't know for sure. If he is, it would be a miracle to spot him among these hordes of people."

Frantically searching the scene, Helena knew the situation was hopeless. She grabbed her sons firmly with each hand and crossed over to catch the number eighteen tram. They all sat in silence, listening to the excited talk of the other riders.

When they got off the streetcar, Helena gathered Hektor and Albert into her arms and then touched her slightly rouged lips with her right index finger. She spoke in a hushed voice.

"Don't ever forget this day and what you just saw. I hope I won't have to send you off to war!"

She dared not say more or say it more loudly; Helena knew how guarded she had to be with the adverse opinions she was known to dispense.

Helena couldn't wait to get home. Her girdle was killing her. She often wondered why she was expected to wear the darn thing. She was slender enough; she certainly didn't feel any need to be corseted. All she needed it for was to hold up her silk stockings. There had to be better means of doing that; a good bra would do the trick in the mammary department.

She put on her comfortable pajamas. Helena undressed the boys and put them to bed. As always, she knelt in prayer with them.

That night her prayers were not only for the safety of her own boys but for all those who had to face the horrors of war. She suddenly became aware of the wetness from her tears. At times Helena began to question if God chose not to answer her prayers. Perhaps the Almighty was too challenged and fatigued facing all the evil visited upon his creation.

As soon as Helena believed her sons to be peacefully asleep, she rose and wiped her face. She walked into the living room and poured herself a sizable snifter of brandy. She sat by the fading warmth of the coal-fired *Kachelofen* [tiled or ceramic heater]. Nursing her sleeping potion, her thoughts were preoccupied with her loved ones' and her own future.

Not in her wildest dreams could she have imagined the outcome of their lives. She had no idea she would never again see her only brother. Three of her cousins would be dead before long. Her beloved Hektor, who couldn't face being separated from her for a single night, would someday cross the Atlantic alone, going off to explore the world and live the balance of his days in the country that would eventually bring an end to the war that had just begun. How could she have known? It was a blessing she didn't fathom all the heartaches that would affect her and her entire family. It was far more than enough for now.

As she took the last swallow of brandy, she rose from her chair and sobbed. Her mind drifted off to *Vom Winde Verweht* [*Gone with the Wind*], the copy of which lay on her night table. It was wrapped in simple brown paper, hiding the title and name of its author. Margaret Mitchell's epic was among many books that had become forbidden fruit in the Third Reich. Helena could not stop herself from quoting her favorite heroine: "I can't face it tonight; I will think about it tomorrow. After all tomorrow is another day!" And with Scarlett O'Hara's famous slogan on her lips, she slumped under the lofty featherbed—alone!

Chapter 2

ON June 22, 1941, Germany invaded Russia. Hektor's father and Helena's cousin, Heinz, belonged to one of the regiments designated to be moved out of Poland in Operation Barbarossa, the massive surprise invasion Hitler planned to launch against his former ally turned foe to the east.

Alex had a short furlough in May 1941, just prior to being moved to Russia. Albert and Hektor wondered what he brought home from the war.

"Dad, what's in the large package you're carrying?"

"Wouldn't you like to know? It's all my dirty laundry I expect your mother to wash for me before I have to leave for the Russian front in a few days."

"Yuk, that sounds gross. Couldn't you get that stuff washed before you came home?"

"Not really, boys. Where we fought, there was no water, never mind a washing machine. But let me show you. I used the dirty clothes as a wrapping."

He laid the mysterious bundle on a table and started to unwrap it. The boys stood there with their mouths wide open. Hektor coughed;

he didn't like the smell drifting off the bundle of his father's dirty clothes. Albert spoke first.

"Oh my God, it's a giant bird with all of its feathers. Where did you get him, or is it a she?" Showing signs of early puberty, Albert had become aware of anatomical differences between boys and girls in his class.

"He ran across my path in Poland and didn't watch where he was going. He didn't look left and right as he was supposed to before he crossed the street. He looked good enough to eat, and I got him with my gun. He rode well hidden in my dirty clothes while I was on the train. It's a good thing I didn't have to travel any farther."

"What kind of a bird is it? We've never seen one that big. He sure doesn't look like a goose."

"They call him a *Puter* or *Truthahn*. Let's get some water boiling; then I'll show you how you boys can help with getting him out of those feathers before your mother gets upset with me for making unnecessary work for her. You know how she is; she doesn't like anything that messes up her kitchen. I've cooked a few of these for my comrades at the front. They like them better than goose. There's a lot more meat, and none of it is as fatty."

Alex found the largest kettle Helena had in her kitchen and brought the water to a boil. He grabbed the bird by its legs, dunking it completely into the boiling water. After doing the job long enough, he tested some of the feathers. When they easily separated from the bird's skin, he knew the boys could help with stripping the huge bird of its plumage.

"It's ready. Come on, boys, let's finish this job before your mother appears. Hektor, don't be afraid. He won't bite. He's long been dead."

"If he wasn't dead, that would hurt." Hektor was hesitant about helping at first.

"It would be worse than pulling hair from your head. Ouch!"

When Helena finally was done with her customers in the store, she walked into her kitchen.

"What do we have here?" Most of the mess had been taken care of, and she saw the gigantic naked bird lying on a platter on her kitchen table.

"Where did you get that critter? I've never seen one that big. Is that what they call a 'turkey' in America? I've read about them but have never seen anything like it. Do you know how to cook it, Alex?"

"Of course I do. I've fixed a few birds for the soldiers in my company. I thought the whole family might enjoy a change from a traditional goose dinner. I think all of you will like it."

Indeed, they all enjoyed the sumptuous meal at the Birkens. By ten in the evening, the last guests had departed; and Helena had put the boys to bed. She said her prayers and made sure they were tucked in under their featherbeds; the boys' room was always cold and damp unless it was beastly hot outside. Helena took her time getting ready for bed. She brushed her teeth, combed her hair, and put on a linen nightgown, selected purposely for its stiffness, not wanting to convey any possible romantic interest. She believed Alex to be long asleep and felt perfectly safe from any sexual advances on his part.

Alex had retired earlier since supposedly he tried to catch up on much-needed sleep. When Helena quietly wanted to slide beneath her featherbed under a cloak of darkness, she found Alex lying on her side of the bed. He had been waiting for her for a long time. First thing he did was to get Helena out of the stiff nightgown. He wanted to enjoy the comfort of holding his wife in his arms. Helena was without words for a second. The last thing she had expected was to be romanced by Alex during this short furlough.

"What do you think you are doing? I'm tired and worn-out from working all day—and now this? Haven't you gotten used to being celibate in the army? Why are you trying to do this to me? You know how I feel about marital relations. I thought I was all done with that."

"Helena, you must be joking. Why are you trying to deprive me of what I enjoy and need? Where did you ever get the idea that my making love to you is something dirty? Most normal couples do it regularly, certainly at our age."

"All right, just do it, and let's get it over with." Helena reluctantly submitted to his romantic advances.

By the time Alex and Cousin Heinz were marching on muddy paths in Russia, Helena knew she was pregnant. She was sorry she went along with Alex in one of her weaker moments. Helena was not thrilled about having to deal with a baby in the midst of war. Her responsibilities were great enough.

During the battles at Brest-Litovsk in late June, Heinz was struck by a grenade. As soon as he was hit, he knew he was in deep trouble. He screamed.

"Help! Help! Someone help me. I can't move."

There were no medics in sight. A couple of his comrades dragged him slowly onto a piece of tarp and moved him out of the line of fire. They were endangering themselves by helping the fallen soldier. He was transported from Russia to a Berlin hospital primarily treating soldiers with spinal cord and cortex injuries. Heinz had become a quadriplegic.

His older brother, Walter, met his mother and cousin Helena at the hospital in Berlin.

"He will never leave this hospital alive" was the assessment of several neurosurgeons they consulted. Walter knew if his brother died there, his brain and spinal cord would be excised for research purposes. Permission to perform such surgery and the removal of body parts was never sought from next of kin.

"Mom, I'll do everything I can to get Heinz moved to a hospital in Essen," Walter assured his mother. Heinz arrived by ambulance at the Huyssenstift hospital in Essen in late August 1941.

"When can we visit Uncle Heinz in the hospital?" Hektor and Albert wanted to know.

Helena wasn't sure how appropriate a visit with the seven-year-old Hektor or the nine-year old Albert would be. Cousin Walter encouraged her.

"Take the boys as often as you can. My brother will love seeing them."

The first visit made for some tense moments. Uncle Heinz, lying flat on his back, could barely turn his head to face his visitors. He smiled when he saw the boys; he was only twenty-one years old. His face had a yellowish tint. Hektor couldn't wait to get away from his uncle.

"Mutti, did Uncle Heinz eat too many lemons? Why's he so yellow looking?" Helena nearly struck her son.

"I'm glad you kept your mouth shut for once; that would have been a terrible thing to ask in front of your ailing uncle. He is very ill; his liver was injured."

"What's a liver?"

"You've seen what a calf's liver looks like in the shop. You've eaten it. It's a very important organ, and Uncle Heinz's was badly hurt. When you are a little older, you'll learn all about it in school. You are too young to understand all of this now. I'm too tired and upset to deal with all your silly questions. Just know your uncle did not eat too many lemons!"

Helena was thankful streetcars and buses were still running. On Sundays they visited Grandma and Grandpa Krämer. It took two streetcars to travel from Essen West to Essen South. Hektor never liked visiting his grandparents. He especially dreaded encounters with his mean grandfather, whose first questions were always aimed at their mother.

"What mischief have the boys gotten themselves into this week? Do I need to use my trusted willow cane and whip their asses into shape?" He wasn't kidding; he often did and seemed to enjoy it. While Hektor liked his grandmother, he couldn't wait to get out of Ratsherrnweg five to visit Cousin Heinz at the Huyssenstift hospital.

It was late November, and Helena and Hektor were on their way home from visiting the ailing uncle. A touch of fresh snow had fallen earlier in the afternoon. Getting on the tram, his mother slipped on one of the icy steps.

"Stop the streetcar," she yelled as she tried to get up in her precarious condition. Others pulled the emergency cord. The conductor realized something seriously wrong had happened.

Helena was seven-months pregnant and knew she was in trouble when her abdomen struck the metal step with extreme force. Within weeks, it was determined the unborn child had died as a result of the unfortunate accident. It was forcefully removed at a local hospital during a bombing. Helena almost bled to death. Hektor had looked forward to having a younger sibling.

"Will there be another baby?"

"I doubt it; God had good reason for taking this one home. I guess it will be just Albert and you. My life is too full as it is; I don't see a way for another baby in this crazy, war-torn world. And don't ask any more questions today. I just can't think about it right now." Hektor was waiting for Scarlett's well-used slogan.

Days after losing the baby, Helena got more bad news. Cousin Walter contracted sepsis. He died on March 3, 1942. The family was devastated.

Uncle Wally was the first dead person Hektor laid eyes on. Helena took the boys to see their uncle for a last time at the large hall of the dead at the Parkfriedhof. His uncle's yellowish, waxlike face frightened him. He didn't dare ask any more questions about the dead person's appearance. He hadn't forgotten the tongue-lashing he'd gotten a few weeks earlier. Adults in the family were kissing the uncle goodbye by touching their lips to his forehead. No way was he going to follow their example.

"Mom, I'm so scared seeing all of this. I actually feel like laughing, although I am not really happy. I am very sad and want to say goodbye to Uncle Wally, but I don't want to kiss him." At first his mother was angry, then she was puzzled. She finally understood the boy's confusion: Hektor encountered death for the very first time. Wanting to laugh in the presence of death was clearly a nervous reaction.

Two days later Hektor stood with his family by the gravesite, watching the lowering of the coffin into the ground. Everyone tossed a shovelful of dirt onto the casket. The hollow sound bouncing off the wooden cover seemed eerie and frightening to Hektor. He did what the adults showed him to do. The boy couldn't wait to be alone with his mother.

"Why are they doing that? It sounds terrible when that hard earth hits the box. It might wake up Uncle Wally." Helena raised an eyebrow. Almost cynically, she spoke against her better judgment.

"I didn't realize Jesus was present at the gravesite." She tried using suitable language.

"It's a custom that people have practiced since time immemorial. I mean, for a long time. In Christian burials, it seems to confirm the pronouncement that we came from dust and are returned to dust." Helena knew immediately that those were not the right words to use with her young boy.

"Some day you will understand all these things. Please, no more questions about Uncle Wally's funeral."

At first no one had the heart to tell Heinz his older brother had passed away. Alas, several days after the funeral, his mother broke the news. Aunt Marla held her son's cold and clammy hands. She was shaking. He shed some tears and said little to comfort his mother, knowing all too well he would be next.

Uncle Heinz died on April 21, 1942, exactly seven weeks after his brother. The family was crushed by the loss of two of its youngest members. Hektor felt traumatized by another death in the family. The outpouring of tears at the Reuter grave shook everyone to the core.

Helena often said she was happy not to know what the future might hold. Alex was seriously injured in late July 1942, during the early skirmishes leading up to the Battle of Stalingrad. He was transported to a war hospital in Baden-Baden. Helena's brother went MIA just outside of Stalingrad, during the winter months. Helena's dire predictions of the impact of war were becoming reality as the conflict continued.

There were days when Helena wondered how much more she could handle. The war casualties began to mount. She blatantly resisted fascist actions. Helena saw too many of her close friends and neighbors disappear. Her father had numerous Jewish friends and business associates. Helena had grown up with their children. They had celebrated their respective holidays together. They were her extended family. Helena had heard they were being sent to some camps. She didn't know where they were being taken. She was threatened with incarceration whenever she openly opposed the regime.

Helena took everything in stride. She succeeded in pawning the boys off with her parents for a couple of days. A quick trip to Baden-Baden was the order of the day. Her outlook on life had hardened during the war years, accounting for her often being flagrantly blunt in her speech.

"You don't look the worse for wear. I can't really feel sorry for you having to lie on your ass all day." She winked at Alex. Both Alex and his roommate, Rudi, were astonished when Helena arrived on the scene totally unannounced.

Knowing Alex was well taken care of, she returned to her battle station in Essen. The bombings of the city steadily increased. Helena kept her emporium of foods going. Her distaste for the German government deepened. Looking across the street at her Jewish neighbors, she heard and saw how the Nazis treated them. The Brownshirts broke into their homes. They robbed their victims blind and burned in the streets what didn't meet with their wants, needs, or approval. Broken glass covered the sidewalks. They yanked Frau Rosenstock by her hair out of her home and literally threw her in the back of their vehicle. Helena's friends and neighbors were hauled away worse than hogs or cattle. There was no longer any human decency. One day she faced two French POWs in the store.

"Je vous remercie! Thank you for bricking in my windows once again. Here is a little more bread and some salami. I'd give you more, but I'm being watched at all times. I hope it helps. Perhaps some Russian soul does the same for my lost brother."

The next day a Belgian and a Dutch POW were standing in line with German patrons who were there to buy the bread Helena had received earlier. She wasn't even certain if she should call it bread. It seemed like it was baked with sawdust rather than flour.

With some importance, a Brownshirt entered the store. He took cuts ahead of the others who patiently stood in line. He reached over the partition separating the customers from Helena. With a flourish, he presented a large leather-bound volume and opened it to a particular page.

"What are you doing, if I may ask?" Helena faced her nemesis. Her tone was bitter.

"I am presenting you with an opportunity to make a major donation to the cause!"

"And which cause might that be?" Helena replied with hate in her voice. She glanced down at the open volume. She recognized her name among a list of other businesspeople. The Nazis had written a donation in the amount of 250 Reichsmarks next to her name. Her face turned purple.

"Where do you people get the nerve to tell me how much of a donation I should give to your cause—if any?"

"Ma'am, we are allowing you to continue operating a successful business during this war. We are loaning you our prisoners of war at no charge to make necessary repairs after any bombings. What we are asking for is a little compensation for all the benefits you gain through government protection."

"Humbug! Humbug! Humbug!" Helena shook her right fist into the Nazi's face. He backed away from her, thankful she hadn't reached for the knife lying on the counter.

"You have no idea how angry you make me. You are not protecting me or my family from anything. You are trying to rob me blind. Why do you think I'm running this business? I cannot feed and house my family on the pittance you are paying my husband for his services to the cause."

The Brownshirt and the others stood there, anchored to the floor. Helena reached into the right pocket of her spotlessly white smock and then opened a drawer under the cash register.

"Where is my red pen? I'll take care of this right away."

Holding the red pen firmly in her right hand, she drew a double line through the predetermined amount. The patrons and the Brownshirt gasped. In her inimitable handwriting, she added a personal note to the insult.

"My donation to Herr Hitler and the Third Reich lies in the Badischer Hof in Baden-Baden!" She turned toward the "gentleman," handing him the elegant book with a flourish.

"Here you are. Sorry, I refuse to call you sir." Her gesture of returning the book was punctuated by a loud slap upon closing it.

Helena conveyed a finality to her action none had expected. As the Brownshirt made his quick exit, everyone heard him mumbling.

"If nothing else, I'll see to it that obnoxious bitch lands in a camp! I'll make damn sure she'll get what she decerves—and real soon." Helena didn't care what the scoundrel had said. She was proud to have stood her ground.

Chapter 3

AFTER the Japanese attack on Pearl Harbor, bombings of strategic targets in Germany gradually became the norm rather than the exception. Essen was the home of the Krupp Works, many coal mines, and much heavy industry producing ammunition, tanks, planes, and U-boats. During 1942, bombings of Essen were a hit-and-miss practice. Now it happened in earnest. The first devastating blow occurred on March 5, 1943.

Helena and her boys emerged from the cellar. The sounds of planes and exploding bombs had finally subsided. Many of the older homes across the street were standing in flames. Civil servants were digging through rubble, searching for bodies. Those who survived the nightmare were anxiously looking at the shrunken and charred remains of their neighbors laid out on the sidewalks. In the haste of the moment, no one had the means or the time to cover the remains with newspaper or a tarp.

"Mom, can we go inside, please? We have seen enough. The stench is awful. What is it?"

Helena didn't want to tell her boys that it was the smell of burning human flesh.

Many schools were destroyed. The city fathers closed them all.

"Take this note to your mother," said Albert's and Hektor's teachers.

"Your parents need to send you away, preferably to small villages in rural areas. If they can't find shelter in the country, the government will send you to Poland, Czechoslovakia, or some other occupied territory. You will be housed in large camps with other displaced children from all over Germany."

Helena was desperate and called her father. She was shaking as she dialed the number, wondering how he would react to what she needed to share with him.

"What shall I do with the boys?"

"You may want to contact my older sisters in Swabia, although they may hesitate to assume responsibility for two young boys at their ages. Better yet, call Alex," he counseled.

She dialed the number at the Badischer Hof.

"I need to speak to my husband, Alex Birken. It is urgent!"

The phone rang in the room occupied by Alex Birken and Rudi Müller. One of the nuns dragged the apparatus from its centrally located table and handed the receiver to Alex.

"Alex Birken speaking." He listened to Helena without wanting to interrupt her. Alex couldn't believe what he was hearing.

"I don't have an answer for you at the moment, but let me think. I'll call you back as soon as I come up with something."

"Well, you better think hard and fast. I'm desperate for a positive and quick answer!" She hung up on him before he could take another breath. Alex turned to his roommate.

"That was Helena. Essen was heavily bombed two nights ago. All schools are closed for the duration of the war. Helena has to find a secure home for the boys—*fast*. You have any ideas, Rudi?"

"Let me call Klara. We have this big old house in a tiny village with less than five hundred people just north of Freiburg. Our house was built in 1495. The enclave isn't exactly a prospective target for bombing."

Rudi's call was a nice surprise for Klara. They didn't often speak on the phone. He did abide by the slogan posted above all public phones in Germany, *"Fasse Dich kurz"* [Keep it short].

"Alex's wife, Helena, has a serious problem. She has to find a home in the country for their two boys. All schools in Essen are closed and will remain so until the war is over. If she's unsuccessful, Albert and Hektor will be at the mercy of the government. What do you think?"

"Refresh my memory. How old are the boys?" Klara inquired in her distinct Badenser dialect.

"The younger of the boys just turned nine; the older one will be eleven in early May."

Klara asked whether the children had ever been away from home. Rudi turned to Alex, posing some of Klara's concerns and questions. After listening carefully to Alex, Rudi shared what he had learned.

"Hektor, the younger boy, was away twice for extended periods. Summer camp, so to speak, or better said, children's homes, did not agree with him at all. The first one he attended when not quite four, and the second at age five. Both times separation anxiety almost did the kid in." Klara began to get antsy.

"That doesn't sound promising to me. And now she wants to send this kid to me, more than five hundred kilometers away from her? You must be joking! What am I supposed to do with a couple of needy boys? I don't even know how to act with kids. As much as I wanted your children, I don't know if I'm equipped to do what you are asking of me."

"The woman is desperate. The kid is four years older. Our home isn't a camp or an institution. Have a heart, Klara. What do you say?"

"It's OK with me. If this Helena person wants to take a chance on me, I'll do anything to make a good home for those boys."

Helena was elated to get the good news. It solved her most imminent problem. Of course, how would she get them to this little town just north of the Black Forest? She didn't know much about that part of the country. Her ancestors came from Swabia rather than Baden.

They had to journey close to five hundred kilometers south. *I won't be able to take them on this trip. Ulrike can't be left alone in the store. Lord knows she might give half the store away for free to her Nazi buddies. Too many people depend on me! I can't send a nine-year-old and an almost eleven-year-old by themselves—or can I? What choice do I have?*

She stopped for a moment. She hadn't even thought about what Hektor's reaction to such a journey would be. *Oh my God, he might die being that far away from me.* Helena felt she needed to talk to her younger son before she made any more plans to ship him off to the country.

"Hektor, come here. Sit with me. You and I need to talk about this trip you are about to take with your brother. Do you have any idea how far away from home you will be?"

"Yes, Mutti, the trip will take us all day. But don't worry; I'm a big boy now. I understand the reasons for sending me away. You cannot help it. Don't cry, Mutti. I will miss you, but I won't be unhappy. I'll be glad not to be running to bomb shelters all the time."

He put his arms around his mother, consoling her. Helena realized for the first time that her kids were growing up. They were no longer her babies, but young boys.

Madame Fiffi, as Georgine dubbed her oldest sister, sprang into action.

"Boys, we have to select what you will take with you. Neither of you can handle a heavy suitcase. I will pack one larger trunk with most of your underwear, heavier clothes, and extra shoes. It's a good thing I will be able to check it through to Köndringen, your final destination. Frau Müller surely will find a way of having someone haul it to her house."

"Did you say that place where we'll be living is almost four hundred fifty years old? I can't imagine what it must be like to live in a house that old."

"Yes, Albert, that's what the man in Dad's hospital room said. He thinks you will be very safe in that little village."

"You think they might have animals?"

"I don't know that for sure, but you'll make some discoveries when you get there. I think it will be important to make things as easy for Frau Müller as we can. I have the name tags that need to be affixed to all your washable stuff. It will be easier to sort through the laundry. Both of you can help me with sewing on all these tags. I'll show you how it's done."

Mother Courage would have been a better name for Helena Birken. She came up with a great idea.

"Boys, I want you to wear these sandwich-board signs hung from your necks. I have written the times and stations where you need to change trains on these boards. Albert, I hold you responsible for your brother. You should have no problems getting to the right trains at the correct locations. Remember, the first change comes rather quickly in Cologne."

)K(

Their journey began on the morning of March 31, 1943. The train blasted its path into the depot.

"Look at all that black smoke coming out of the locomotive. You think it's on fire, Mutti?" Hektor wanted to know.

"No, Hektor, it's just what happens with coal-fired steam engines."

A few tears emerged in all their eyes. They had to be courageous; tears were a sign of weakness. This was wartime. All had to be strong. The train came to a complete stop. The boys hopped on. Each carried his own suitcase and a small satchel. Handkerchiefs were waved from the broad window of the wagon as well as from the platform. They were on their way to the land of escape.

Helena was still standing there as the last of the steam was blown away by a gust of wind. Anxiety gave way to sadness. She felt terribly alone and lost. Tears were flooding her eyes as she mumbled to herself. "What have I done? How could I put my young boys on that train by themselves? My God, if something happens to them, I'll never forgive myself. Why didn't I close that damn store for a few days and take them to that godforsaken village?"

She slowly made her way back to the little Steyr and sobbed as she put her head down on the steering wheel. Their mother was more upset than the boys. They were looking forward to their very first adventure. Albert and Hektor reached the Cologne station forty-five minutes into the journey. As their speedy conveyance steamed into the gigantic Cologne Hauptbahnhof, they spotted the dual spires of the famous cathedral. Albert turned to Hektor.

"Grab your things. This is where we catch the really fast train, the Astral Express. The next stretch will be our longest ride. We won't get off for hours. Maybe we'll have a chance to talk to soldiers riding with us?"

"You think that's a good idea? Mother said we should keep to ourselves and not talk to strangers!"

"Let me handle it. I'm the older one, although I have to admit you are the talker in the family!"

As the Astral Express jerked to a start, Albert remembered their first mission. He had tucked into his satchel their mother's ultimate weapon of punishment—the cat and nine tails. When either of the kids committed a punishable act, their mother visited "the cat" upon both of them. She firmly believed if one needed it, the other was just as deserving. Once she discovered that her sons were prepared for her actions by sticking cardboard in their pants, she made them strip down to their naked butts before she whacked them viciously. The boys were determined to deal with this instrument of torture.

The window of their compartment slid open easily. Accompanied by youthful exuberance, the cat sailed into the air, never to be seen or used again.

The boys were traveling second class. First class was reserved exclusively for high-ranking military and the haute-volée. Third class was too risky for them to travel alone. The compartment door opened. They were facing several boisterous young soldiers.

"Are these seats vacant?"

"Yes sir," said Albert. He had no clue what rank the soldier might be. The soldiers moved right in. Albert was happy to have company other than Hektor.

"Why are you wearing those signs?" one of the soldiers asked.

"We are on our way to some little village north of the Black Forest. We are traveling by ourselves. Our mother runs a grocery store in Essen. She can't get away. Our dad was injured just outside of Stalingrad and is lying flat on his back in Baden-Baden. We won't be seeing him right away. Once we are settled in our new home, we'll visit him. He is only eighty kilometers from where we will live. Our mother thought the signs would help us make the right train connections."

"Pretty smart woman. She had the right idea."

Albert hit Hektor in his side with his right elbow.

"Why are you telling them all those things? We don't know who they are. You just reminded me a short while ago about Mother asking us not to speak to strangers. And what did you do just now? Keep your mouth shut!"

"Sorry! I thought you wanted to be friendly to these guys."

Albert decided to let it be. The humble sandwiches and apples their mother packed were shared. The soldiers, in turn, parted with their rations, which were slightly more intriguing. The boys were bothered by the awful smell of the smokes. They wished the soldiers would light up in the gangway.

By late afternoon they arrived in Karlsruhe. A local train with strange-sounding passengers would take them to Köndringen. After umpteen stops at every little nest, they arrived at the unknown village just before dusk.

"Are you OK, Hektor? Aren't you scared? You usually scream for Mother when it gets dark."

"I'm not scared. I'm a big boy. This will be an adventure."

He was glad Albert didn't want to hold him by his sweaty hands. They had no idea for whom they were looking. As they stepped off the train, a short, stocky woman approached them. Her singsong gibberish sounded more like a foreign language than a variation of German. Hektor looked at Albert.

"Did we accidentally land in Poland?"

Before they could ponder the effect of such an error, Klara Müller spoke.

"Yeeees boyyyyyyys, I'mmm Frau Müller. Welcum, welcum to de laaand of eeeeescape." She was indeed the person for whom they were looking.

Klara was a woman in her late thirties—a few years older than their mother. She had thick dark hair that was twisted into an impressive bun at the back of her neck. Above her smiling mouth, she sported a healthy growth of dark hair. The boys looked at each other and giggled.

"Don't tell her why we are laughing." Albert nudged Hektor.

Frau Müller, as they learned to address her at first, was anxious to get them home. They thought she was saying they needed to go to bed right away after the long day of traveling.

"You've got to be kidding. We are not tired. This is all so new and exciting."

She carried the boys' bags and let them hold on to their small satchels. They walked about a mile or less from the station.

The path took them along a swift-running, rather muddy stream. Soon they passed an old church with an imposing steeple. They turned left past the church and walked through a narrow alley.

"Wow! Look at that gilded lion!"

"That's right. That's where you boys will be living with me. *Zum Löwen* [Lion Inn] will be your home for a while. The Shell gas station is closed for now."

They walked through the imposing five-hundred-year-old arched portal into a courtyard. Albert noticed a trough cut from red sandstone with its hand-operated pump.

"What's that? And for what is it used?"

"Some of my guests arrive on horses. They often like to water them from that vessel."

The entire courtyard was surrounded by giant barns and stone walls. They spotted the tall towers made up of neatly cut wooden strips or planks.

"What are those things for?" they asked.

Frau Müller proudly told them her husband was a cooper or barrel maker by trade.

"When my husband comes back from the war, he will need to make all sorts of new barrels. He will use some of that beautiful wood that is drying out there."

Klara climbed the well-worn stone steps to the ground level. Albert and Hektor followed her, skipping upward easily. They flinched when they heard a racket.

"Look up, boys. Do you see that very large nest on top of the peak at the far end of the church roof? Well, it's a storks' nest. The large bird circling the nest is a male. You are witnessing the annual ritual of the storks' return to their summer abode."

The boys just stood there, fascinated by the deft maneuvers of the giant bird. Then they walked into the huge old kitchen and glimpsed its enormous wood-and-coal-fired stove. There was a pump by an ancient sandstone sink along the wall to their left. Guests were in the pub. A neighbor of Frau Müller's was tending to the patrons.

"Here, let me show you your room up these stairs!" She continued talking in that singsongy, dragged-out voice.

"My neighbor Norbert Böhm will fetch your big suitcase a little later. The stationmaster locked it in the storage room. It will be perfectly safe. Let me help you with your bags."

Albert and Hektor listened to more of her gibberish. Slowly, they made out what Frau Müller was trying to tell them.

They climbed the steep wooden stairway to the second floor. Their bedroom was next door to Klara's. The room was small and had twin beds, one on each wall. There were just a few feet separating the beds. The room was bright and clean. Klara opened the windows. One of them allowed the boys to look out on the main drag, the other into a neighboring farmer's courtyard. Country air wafted through the open windows.

"Smell that, Hektor. Having grown up on a farm, Grandpa used to call that 'prosperity.'"

They listened very closely, hoping to grasp what the woman was trying to tell them.

"The house is almost five hundred years old. There is no indoor plumbing. The pump in the kitchen is the only source of water inside the house. Wait until you use the second-story indoor outhouse. Don't be shocked by the sound when your poop hits the water. You'll get used to it. When you boys or any guys from the inn need to pee, use the outdoor pissoir. It's easier on the holding tank. It's a good thing I rarely have women in the guesthouse. They have to use the upstairs potty room. What do you think so far?"

"It's different, for sure," voiced Albert.

Klara pointed out the upstairs root cellar. Dried and some fresh fruits were stored there. The boys were intrigued by the long strings of dehydrated apple rings and pear slices that hung from the low ceiling.

"What are those little bites on the fruit?"

"Boys, the mice in the house have to eat too." They looked at one another with saucer-sized eyes.

"Mice?" Hektor commented.

"Mother wouldn't stay here for any reason. We know how scared she is of mice!"

They dropped off their things in their room and joined Klara in the pub.

"These are my visitors from the big city of Essen. They will be with me for a while. Their mother sent them by railway, and they made it all alone. Their mom and dad should be proud of them."

The guys sitting around the *Stammtisch* [a large table always reserved for regular locals] applauded the boys. Klara let them fend for themselves while she went to the kitchen to fix liver with onions and wild mushrooms, a hearty meal after the long trip. They discovered the first night she was a pretty good cook. After supper, Albert got Frau Müller's attention.

"May we make a quick call to our mother. She said she would be more than happy to reimburse you. We'll keep it real short; we know it isn't cheap to make long-distance calls."

Remembering how the boys had reacted to her speech earlier, Klara made a concerted effort to sound a bit more *hochdeutsch* [high German].

"Naturally, naturally. Why didn't I think of that as soon as you got here? We'll have to use this coin-operated phone by the bar. I have plenty of change. And tell your mother not to worry about reimbursing me. It's my pleasure to have you boys with me!" Hektor and Albert liked her already.

Klara pulled a bunch of coins out of the cash register and walked over to the phone. "Can you men keep down the noise a little? These boys want to call their mom." The phone rang in Essen.

"Birken Groceries, Helena speaking."

"Hallo, Frau Birken. It's Klara Müller calling from Köndringen. The boys have arrived safely. They just ate and wanted to speak with you. Here is Albert."

"Hallo, Mutti. We are here. It was a long but wonderful ride. We met some friendly soldiers on the Astral Express from Cologne to Karlsruhe. Oh, and we like our room. Hektor is planning to write to you as often as he can. It will be cheaper to write than to call. You know he loves to write, and he writes a lot. Here he is now. He wants to say good night to you."

"Thanks, Albert. Be good!"

"Hallo, Mutti! I unpacked my satchel and found the new diary you sent. I promise I will write in it every day. Thank you so much. I think there will be lots of new and exciting adventures to record. I will write you tomorrow."

"It's wonderful to hear your voices, boys. I'm so happy you got there safely, and I'm looking forward to your letters, Hektor."

"I miss you, Mutti, but I won't cry. I've grown up, Mutti! And have I traveled! I love you very much. Be safe, and always go down to the cellar as soon as you hear the sirens sound. Good night!"

"Good night, Hektor. Sleep well." He hesitated to break the connection.

"Thank you, Frau Müller, for letting us speak to our mother. My brother and I are very tired. Let us say good night for now," offered Albert.

Retiring to their bedroom, Albert and Hektor felt heat coming from the tiled wall; it was generated by a Kachelofen fired in Frau Müller's bedroom. With their tummies filled and their minds saturated with new and exciting impressions, the boys climbed under the giant featherbeds and were asleep before saying another word to each other.

Chapter 4

LATER the next day, Hektor started to make his initial entry in his diary. He asked Klara for paper and carbon, allowing him to send his mother a copy of his entries. This way he wouldn't have to write everything twice. He thought that was pretty clever for a kid his age.

It was good speaking with Mother last night. We had quite the trip. It wasn't boring at all. We loved the Astral Express and the speed at which we traveled. The soldiers we met shared some of their army rations with us. Talk about different food. When we arrived in Köndringen, we weren't sure at first that we were at the right village. The people, including Frau Müller, speak so differently than us. Guess we'll get used to that.

This morning we got up real early. We learned that the inn is always closed on Thursdays. Frau Müller rides her bike to Emmendingen to get her hair done. It takes her about two hours to do that.

We are not starting school until next week. We asked her if there was anything we could do to stay out of trouble. It is a big house, and there are lots of things for us to explore. She has all kinds of rabbits. Some of them are really cute and cuddly. She told us that she cleaned all the rabbit hutches just yester-day. Her critters are enjoying the clean straw and look well fed. She expects us to do some of these jobs in the future.

Mutti, you'd be scared in this old house. Frau Müller told us she doesn't mind the mice living with her.

She finally asked us if we had ever cleaned a pigsty. We didn't even know what she was talking about. We told her neither one of us had ever done anything like that before, but it sounded like a different kind of escapade to us.

Frau Müller showed us where the hogs were housed. The pigpen was right between the pissoir [that's a place outside where the men and boys piss against the wall—and it stinks!] and the washroom where the laundry is boiled, the Kirschwasser [clear brandy] is secretly processed in a still, and all in the family take their weekly baths. That was a lot of new information.

We really had to listen carefully to understand all that she was trying to tell us. She's a nice lady, but Mutti, she does talk fast and sounds funny to us.

She told us about the hot water in the large copper kettle; she had done laundry chores long before we got up. We were to use the hot water left in the washroom to scrub the floor of the pigsty. The water was plenty soapy. Frau Müller had used it to boil the white linens. She didn't think it would hurt the hogs at all. She warned us to be careful when draining the water into a bucket. The water was still pretty hot. The copper kettle retains the heat well. With those final words, she hopped on her bike and left us alone.

The courtyard is completely enclosed and very safe. We let the two hogs run freely; they seemed to enjoy themselves despite the nippy weather. Albert did the bit with the pitchfork and got rid of most of the dirty straw.

We took off our shoes and socks. It was easier to wash our feet when we were done with the mess. You know that I don't like to do messy jobs. Boy, and this was a doozy. It will take some getting used to being so close to animals.

Albert poured a couple of buckets of hot water on the floor, and I used a big push broom and swept out the dirty water. The new straw was light in weight. I had no trouble spreading it on the clean floor.

We tried doing a good job of cleaning the sty; then we looked at the pigs and saw how dirty they were. We thought they needed a scrubbing as well. Albert was game to catch the hogs one at a time. He found a couple of heavy chains in the washroom. Catching those buggers and tying their front and hind legs was another story. But he did it! I'm glad he is as strong as he is.

Albert and I worked real hard and scrubbed each hog with hot, soapy water. The tiny black specks in the hogs' skin didn't want to come out. We wondered why the pigs were squealing so loudly. We thought they would be happy to be really clean for once. Albert and I certainly wouldn't want to get into a clean bed if we were as filthy as those pigs. Finally, we gave up on those little black specks and released them into their fresh pen. The pigs looked nice and pink but were shaking wildly as they cuddled next to each other in the clean straw.

When Frau Müller got back, we let her know what a fine job we had done on cleaning our first pigsty. She smiled until I spoke up and told her we had scrubbed the pigs as well.

She screamed in horror, "You what?" Frau Müller thought we might have killed her hogs. She rushed to the pigsty, only to discover her four-legged friends were still alive, although obviously suffering from the cold. She quickly secured old blankets and rushed in with an electric heater; she hung it from the ceiling, connecting it to an old extension cord. She was hoping not to set the stall on fire in the process of rescuing her suffering pigs. The hogs were literally saved by her swift action.

Frau Müller didn't know what she would have done had they succumbed to the cold. She couldn't call a butcher to perform emergency slaughter. She is raising those hogs on the sly; no one is allowed to have any livestock for personal consumption right now. Needless to say, we would have been in deep doo-doo. And, of course, we hadn't planned it to be an April first prank.

Helena wrote back and let them know how excited she was to hear of their first-day adventures in Köndringen and reminded both boys to be on their best behavior since Mrs. Müller was having them there out of the goodness of her heart. She let them know that she was keeping herself very busy with the store and on weekends visited uncles and aunts and, of course, Grandma and Grandpa. Everyone in the family was sending them their love.

Albert and Hektor met their next-door neighbors, Frau Böhm and her son, Norbert, a few days later. He was several years older than Albert. Norbert helped his widowed mother with their farming chores, although he was slightly handicapped. His older brothers were all conscripted.

Mrs. Böhm appeared to be a kind old lady. She made quite a striking figure in her long, flowing black outfits. Her hair was snow white and twisted in a heavy knot at the back of her head. Outside the home, her head was always covered with a black shawl. Even when she crossed the courtyard from the house to the barn, she was never seen in anything but her black widow's garments. Mrs. Böhm wore her black cloak milking the cows, working the fields, or tending the grapevines in the hills. It made no difference how hot or cold a day it was—her stark garb of widowhood was worn with dignity.

The boys started school on Monday, April 5, 1943. The school was just a block from the Lion Inn and across the street. A big photo of Adolf Hitler hung behind the desk of their teacher, Herr Herb. He lost his right arm in World War I and thus was excused from serving in the army. He wore one of those Swastika bands on his left arm. Herr Herb gave instructions to the new kids.

"When you boys enter or leave the classroom, I expect you to face Adolf Hitler's photograph, click your heels together, raise your right arm, extending your hand, and shout *Heil Hitler.* Do you understand me?"

"Yes, Herr Herb, we'll do exactly as you showed us!" With that, they faced Hitler and raised their right hands in a salute to the leader.

Both boys were in the same class. Three grades were clustered due to the lack of teachers. Hektor had no trouble keeping up with the higher grades in subjects like reading, writing, and arithmetic. The sciences were slightly more challenging; he just had to study harder.

The school building was modern, as were most houses built on that side of the road. The Lion Inn was among some of the oldest buildings in the village. In front of those older farmhouses ran a smelly drainage ditch. Luckily, when they built the Shell station in front of the Lion Inn, the ditch was replaced with underground sewer pipes. They couldn't figure out what that awful smell was as they were walking to school that first day. One of the local kids set them straight.

"What you are smelling is seepage from holding tanks filled with human and animal piss and shit."

After that, they crossed the street as soon as they left the Lion Inn for school. It was a good thing they had gotten into the habit of doing so right from the beginning.

A few days after starting school, a very long truck entered the village on the way south. The driver was hauling umpteen large drums filled with dangerous chemicals. The drums were held down with rusty old chains that broke just as he passed the school. The drums rolled off the truck and landed in the ditch. Had the kids not been walking on the sidewalk in front of the newer houses, the falling drums might have mowed them down.

Most mornings, when they got up early, there was a wonderful earthy fragrance in the air. The city slickers were clearly aware of cows, horses, and goats living next door to them. Frau Müller opened the inn at seven thirty every day but Thursdays.

Some farmers came in for a shot and a warmed beer before tending to their livestock and heading out to the grape arbors or their fields of wheat and maize. Warming the beer was news to the boys. They remembered how they had to use a special *Krug* [jug] when getting beer for Grandpa at the corner pub. He wanted to be sure the beer stayed cold. Things were different in Köndringen—that was for sure.

The kids got to know some of the regular early customers and knew what they liked. While Frau Müller fixed breakfast, the two of them took turns at handling the bar. The first time Hektor tried to operate the spigots, he learned that he was too short to properly draw a beer.

"Get on that footstool," yelled Albert. "Then you can reach the spigot."

"I will, I will, but that thing is so wobbly. I'm afraid I might fall right off the darn thing!"

"You won't; just hold on to the spigot with your free hand!"

Soon they knew how to do the job perfectly. By raising the tall glasses up and down and slightly tilting them during the process, they were able to create a respectable head of foam on the beer and filled the glasses to just the right level. The beer was very cold since the barrels were stored in one of the caverns underneath the ancient inn. For those of the early-morning patrons who asked to have their draft warmed a tad, they immersed the electric coil into the ale until the desirable temperature was attained.

Helena was glad to learn that the boys had missed the terrible accident in the village. She also let them know that she was seriously pursuing the building of a much safer bomb shelter in her basement.

Hektor didn't run out of stories to record in his diary and share with his mother. It seemed like there were all sorts of exciting things happening during their first month in Köndringen.

He was all excited about the creation of the beautiful Maypole by the villagers. The celebration was a lot more colorful and fun than the parades of workers and boring speeches back home in Essen. After being there for a couple of months, Hektor and his brother were beginning to sound more and more like the locals.

Chapter 5

THEY had a big surprise the first weekend in May. The doctors in Baden-Baden thought Herr Müller well enough to come home for an extended weekend. He discovered that his Kirschwasser supply was running low. The kids had no clue what he was talking about when he mentioned the "magic" of Kirschwasser.

"Some day when you are older, boys, you'll discover what it is all about." Since he was still quite handicapped, Herr Müller enlisted their help on several jobs involving the elixir.

"Your first job will be to carry many buckets of fermented cherries from the cellar to the washhouse. I'm still limping badly and need to rely on your help."

"You mean you want us to carry that stinking stuff from the cellar? Is that what you need to make the Kirschwasser? Yuk!" said both Hektor and Albert.

But the boys were eager to be of assistance. Rudi seemed to be a real nice guy. They loved listening to his soft and pleasing speech. They had a much easier time understanding Rudi than his wife.

"Since you boys are doing such a great job working with me, how would you like to go to the circus tonight?"

"We'd love it. It's something we always wanted to experience but never had the chance at home. No one dared set up a big top in Essen after the war began."

After all that stuff was brought to a boil in the copper kettle, they couldn't believe the stench in the washhouse. Albert and Hektor didn't understand how anyone could like drinking that "wonderful" Kirschwasser. Mr. Müller kept saying they would like it when they were older. Albert was wondering how old he had to be before he could test the waters.

"Boys, we are far from done! You'll need to shed all your clothes except your skivvies and get inside the huge barrel and scrub it real hard until it is super clean. Try to do as good a job as you did on the pigs."

Obviously, his wife had told him the story of the clean pigs.

Rudi proceeded to treat the barrel with strips of sulfur.

"What is that awful smell?" Albert wanted to know.

Both Albert and Hektor pinched their noses. Luckily, they were outside the barrel by then. Rudi explained to the boys the importance of sterilizing the barrel.

As the sun began to set, they were all done with smelly jobs, and Rudi gave them the money to see the circus.

"Did you say we have to walk five kilometers into Emmendingen? That's a long way on an unknown road!"

"Yes, boys, if you want to see the circus. Also, you will have to walk back in the dark. Are you sure you want to do this on your own? You are not afraid of the dark, are you?"

"Oh no. We aren't afraid of anything!"

Speak for yourself! Hektor thought.

"Remember, boys, you cannot use flashlights, because of the total blackout conditions," Klara reminded them.

Suddenly they weren't so sure any longer about walking the dark road for five kilometers. When they got to the circus, they couldn't believe how well everything was blacked out. There wasn't even light shining through the circus tent. They had fun watching the exotic people and animals. The walk home along the country road in pitch darkness was scary, but they made it. Rudi and Klara had waited up for them.

"Well, how was the circus? Did you have fun?" explored Rudi.

"Oh, we did have fun! The elephants and the people flying through the air near the top of the tent were my favorites," said Hektor.

"The walk home was kind of scary. We've never done anything like it at home. We are glad you waited up for us, and thanks again for letting us go to the circus. I had fun too," shared Albert.

"You boys better get to bed since you plan to attend church tomorrow. I won't be going with you. I'll try to finish making the Kirschwasser since I'm supposed to head back to Baden-Baden on Tuesday, but I want to stay around for Albert's eleventh birthday on Monday."

)|(

Frau Müller made Albert's favorite breakfast—blood sausage and pancakes from grated raw potatoes. He was happy with the package his mother had sent. He really could use the socks she knitted. Most of the time they went barefoot, except when going to church. Walking on gravel was painful, but thankfully they were slowly getting callused feet.

When they sat down for lunch, Albert had disappeared.

"Hektor, where is your brother?" asked Rudi.

"Sorry, I haven't seen him since noon. He was using the pissoir last time I saw him outside."

They searched everywhere and finally found him in the washhouse, lying in front of the still. He was delirious and scared the heck out of the Müllers. Rudi yelled at Klara.

"Call the doctor. This kid is in deep shit! I'd make a wager that Albert drank the elixir straight from the still and is suffering from alcohol poisoning."

Klara did as told and reported to the doctor what they thought might have happened.

"You know what to do. Have Rudi haul him over to Böhms, and get him ready for burial. I'll be there as soon as possible."

Hektor was astounded by what they wound up doing to his delirious brother. Herr Müller carried him over to the neighbors, momentarily forgetting about his limp and cane. The neighbors dug a huge hole in their pile of cow manure and were getting ready to bury Albert in the dung. He was stripped down to nothing. His face and his ears were the only parts not covered with poop. He was in that pile of manure for close to two hours. If he wasn't before, he now found himself indeed in deep shit. Eventually, he came to.

"I hope I don't have to be involved in another stinking job—and especially not on my birthday."

All were happy to hear his bitching. If the burial in poop hadn't sobered him, what followed certainly did the job.

"You must be crazy; don't use that hose. That water is ice cold." But Norbert kept working the pump as fast as he could while Rudi hosed Albert down from head to toe.

"Never again drink straight from a still, and forget about drinking any alcohol as long as you are still green behind your ears," warned the doctor.

After Herr Müller gave Albert a hot bath in the washhouse, the boy ran for the closest mirror. He never did find the green behind his ears the doctor had mentioned. Neither Albert nor any of the others ever forgot his eleventh birthday.

)(

After hearing of Albert's close call with destiny, Helena wasn't so sure about wanting to hear any more adventure stories from Köndringen. She was happy to report that she was proceeding with building the new bomb shelter with the help of her prospective brother-in-law, Franz Dimmelsburg.

Chapter 6

THE summer of 1943 in the village of Köndringen was a fun time. The little village lies at the foot of the *Kaiserstuhl*. The entire region is considered the fruit basket of Germany. The gentle hills were saturated with grape arbors and the valleys covered by millions of fruit trees. The spectacular blossom time of spring gave way to trees burgeoning with cherries, plums, peaches, apples, and pears. They ripened in their good time before the grape harvest in late fall would signal the end of another fruitful year. The year 1943 was no exception.

Summer vacation meant freedom from studying and regular all-day presence at the country schoolhouse. It did not necessarily mean idleness for most children. Hektor and Albert learned that lesson fast.

Frau Müller owned a tract of land on the outskirts of the neighboring village of Heimbach. She and the boys would trek to the plot. Each of them would carry a spade and rake over their shoulders and march in single file along the country road. Sometimes a farmer would offer a ride on an oxen-drawn cart. That would make the distance of a few kilometers more palatable, especially carrying the garden tools, lunch, and whatever.

First the entire area was turned over and prepared for the seeds, and before long it would be time to weed and water all they had planted. As soon as poppies started blooming, the boys became curious.

"What are these funny flowers and these capsules developing?

"Those are poppies. Please do not play with them, and don't stick the pods or the seeds in your mouth. You might become dizzy or even sick. Later you can taste some of those seeds on my sticky buns. That will be OK."

"What do you mean by getting dizzy? Is that like the stuff I drank from the machine in the washroom?"

"Yes and no. It's different. I don't want to take the time to explain it to you right now. Just believe me and do as I say. Stay away from those capsules!"

"Yes, Aunt Klara!"

The highlight of the summer vacation was a visit to see their father at the hospital in Baden-Baden. When they visited him, he was in good spirits. They laughed a lot with him and Uncle Rudi about some of the stuff they had done since living with Aunt Klara. A few weeks into their stay, the boys made up their minds—they would rather call them uncle and aunt instead of Herr and Frau Müller. All were favorably impressed by the boys' choice; they felt like family for the first time.

One of the funniest things were the outfits the nuns at their dad's hospital wore. They were Cistercian nuns. The headgear was boatlike and absolutely gigantic. Neither Hektor nor Albert could keep their eyes from staring at those canal boats on top of the nuns' heads. Hektor planned to talk about it during show-and-tell at school when they returned from their summer vacation—not that their Nazi teacher would have liked talking about Catholic nuns.

The boys were happy that their mother was moving ahead with the improved bomb shelter and that she obviously enjoyed working with Aunt Georgine's future husband on the project. They were looking forward to seeing their mother during a visit to Baden-Baden, as was Aunt Klara. This would be the first face-to-face meeting of Klara and Helena since the boys had come to live in Köndringen.

Midsummer brought the cherry-picking season. Of course, Hektor and Albert were involved with helping their neighbors. They liked wearing the kidney-shaped baskets when climbing the ladder in those big old cherry trees. They learned a hard lesson.

"Boys, if I were you, I would take the time and spit out those cherry pits. I speak from personal experience many years ago," Norbert suggested.

The boys chose not to listen to his advice and thought it was a waste of time to spit out the little buggers; they continued to swallow them. When they were hit by a variant of Montezuma's revenge, they almost didn't make it to the indoor outhouse at the Lion.

Another new experience involved becoming acquainted with a strange-shaped thing growing in abundance in the backyard of the Lion. A bright yellow fruit resembling a pepper or a misshapen apple had caught their eyes.

"Albert have you noticed those funny-looking bright yellow apples on that tree in the backyard? It's that one closest to the church wall. I sure would like to see what it tastes like."

"Be my guest. You know me and tasting strange foods. I am a lot pickier than you when it comes to unknown solid matter. I'm more adventurous when it comes to liquid stuff, as you well remember."

Hektor reached up to the tree, feeling for a moment like Eve reaching up to the forbidden fruit. Biting into one of these tempting apples was indeed a bitter lesson learned. All Hektor could yell was "Yuck" as he spit out what was in his mouth and pitched the dregs as far as he could. Just then, Aunt Klara walked into the yard, wishing to pick fresh herbs for the evening meal. She caught Hektor retching and spitting out the bitter yellow fruit.

"You cannot eat quince like an apple. But quince make a tasty jam, which I will let you sample. Later we will harvest the fruit and make the marmalade. I saved a lot of my rationed sugar for this purpose. Few people have quince trees; I use the fruit for bartering or trading with friends and neighbors. They share some of their other jams and jellies or their sugar rations with me."

Chapter 7

ON July 2, 1943, the phone rang at the Lion Inn. It was Helena calling to let Aunt Klara know that she would be arriving in Baden-Baden on the morning of the third. She had made arrangements to stay at a small pension near the Badischer Hof.

"Klara, I would like it if Hektor and Albert would meet me and their father later tomorrow morning after my arrival. I believe it is important for me to make an appearance."

"That sounds urgent. Is anything wrong, Helena?"

"I'll tell you all about it when we meet. I'm thrilled with Rudi's offer to store most of our valuable things at the Lion for the duration of the war. I need to buy some decent clothes for the boys and hope to do so in Baden-Baden. There's another matter. I'd rather talk about it in person after we've met. I'm really pissed at my husband. Well, we'll talk soon. Thanks for everything."

"You are most welcome, Helena. I love having your boys with me. They've given me something I never thought I would live to see. I'll experience much heartache when the time comes to turn them back to you in the future. Till later." Helena hung up the phone. She started to sob thinking about what Klara had said about her boys.

Helena wanted to ascertain the truth as to a suspected affair Alex was having with a civilian nurse at the war hospital. She couldn't believe what she inferred from something Alex let slip during a recent telephone call. *He wouldn't have a dalliance with one of the nuns, or would he?* That would have been the ultimate insult.

Hektor and Albert met their mother at the pension. She marched them right over to the Badischer Hof. As always, she met her challenge head-on. Helena didn't care who would hear her. She was lucky none of the nuns were in earshot.

"If you want to carry on an affair with some hussy here at the hospital, go right ahead. Just don't expect me to take this kind of behavior lying down. While you are supposedly resting your injured bones in this fancy hospital, I am keeping the home fires burning. I can't even imagine you having sex with anyone in your condition. You must be desperate. I certainly did not expect to be defeated and betrayed by my own husband. I have half a mind to leave you. If it wasn't for the boys, I wouldn't think about it twice." Hektor and Albert weren't quite certain what Helena meant.

"Sorry, Rudi. Thanks for offering to store our things at the Lion for the duration of the war. I look forward to meeting Klara tomorrow and to see with my own eyes where the boys landed a few months ago. You two were a Godsend in troubled times. I truly don't know how we will ever be able to thank you. You and Klara are a gift." Rudi just smiled and winked at her.

"Glad to be of help. You certainly have your hands full. Klara loves having the boys with her. She has no problem with giving up one of the guest rooms to store your valuables." She drew the curtain around Alex's bed and walked over to give Rudi a hug.

"Thanks, Rudi for all you and Klara have been willing to do for us." She grasped both of his hands and almost reached out to give him another hug.

"Boys, let's get the heck out of this darn place; I want to get you some new clothes in one of these elegant shops. Just look at you in those tired old rags! I'm hoping to find something halfway decent for our ration stamps."

Helena walked out of the room without giving Alex a backward glance. She and the boys did their shopping, and Mother Birken was pleased with the things she was able to purchase.

"You will stay with me at the pension, and we'll have dinner there tonight. We are leaving for Köndringen first thing in the morning. If you want to say goodbye to your father and Uncle Rudi, do as you see fit. I'm not setting foot in that place again, fancy Cistercian nuns and all. To me, it has become a den of iniquity." The boys were wondering what kind of a den their mother had in mind.

Early in the morning, they were on the train to Köndringen. Aunt Klara greeted them with open arms.

"Welcome, Helena, welcome! You and the boys are a sight for sore eyes. So happy to finally meet you. I just love having your boys with me. So glad we have dispensed with any formalities. Let me take you upstairs, Helena, and show you your quarters. The boys' room is small, as is mine. None of us seem to mind. All we do there is sleep.

"Rudi has spoken to me about his suggestion for you to store your things here until the end of the war. Let me show you the rooms I have in mind." After walking down a long hallway leading to the former dance hall, she unlocked a door.

"This is the largest of the guest rooms in the inn. Do you believe it will accommodate all the belongings you wish to ship?" Helena gave the room a quick once-over.

"Yes, it will do just fine. We probably can set up the beds. The wardrobe and the large buffet are the other large pieces. My sewing machine can stand over there next to all sorts of boxes holding, china, silver, linens, and most of my library. The little vitrine, which will be empty, could stand over there. The dining room table can shed its legs, and all chairs could be stacked and nested in that corner. I can see all of it fitting in here. It's a very good-sized room. Are you sure you can afford to give up this nice room for storage purposes?"

"Helena, don't even fret about it. Remember, these are war times. I don't have many travelers coming this way these days. Did you notice the gas station is closed? There is no petrol available in this area. The few businessmen who stop here now and then will be happy with anything I have to offer. Most of them are *alte Knacker* [old geezers] who are happy with anything I have to offer.

"Let me put you in touch with Herr Spandau in Emmendingen. He can make all the arrangements from this end. He certainly will have ways of getting in touch with professional colleagues in Essen and arrange for the move of your things as quickly as possible. I just pray that all this will happen before you lose everything." Walking back toward the staircase, a small mouse ran across Helena's feet. She shrieked and almost lost her balance.

"My God, Klara. I didn't believe Hektor when he wrote about the mice in the house. You don't seem to be disturbed at all."

"Helena, remember we live in the country and in an almost-five-hundred-year-old house. And also, as courageous as you are in everything else, how can you be so frightened by a little mouse? The mice are afraid of us; just learn to ignore them." Mother Birken kept shaking her head as she walked down the steps. It was all settled.

"What was the other matter you wanted to discuss with me in person? Was there something wrong with Alex?"

"Darn tooting, there's something wrong. I don't know how he does it lying flat on his back. Apparently, he's been screwing around with one of the civilian nurses at the hospital. I assume it was a civilian rather than one of the nuns. Wouldn't that be a slap in my Protestant face? They must have done it quietly behind the drawn privacy curtain or when Rudi was out cold."

"I can't believe it. He must be really horny. I'm glad Rudi comes home once in a while."

"Well, let's drop it. I made no bones about it in front of Rudi or the boys. I hope Alex got my message!"

Helena met with Herr Spandau early on Monday morning. She was impressed with his professional conduct and his willingness to put the whole process in motion. He estimated that all could be situated at the Lion Inn in no more than three weeks. Helena was elated.

She departed on the next available train to Essen. In her opinion, it was a short but successful visit. She hoped to have taught Alex a lesson, loved Rudi and Klara for what they were willing to do for her and her children, and liked the quaintness of the little village that gave safe shelter to her boys. The mice she could live without.

Chapter 8

In mid-July, Rudi returned to the homestead for an extended furlough. His arrival was timed with the height of the cherry harvest. The barrels cleaned and sterilized earlier were now filled to the brim with fresh cherries. Rudi was well satisfied with Klara's negotiations for the fruit; the boys did a great job of filling three huge vessels.

"You boys were a big help to Aunt Klara and me. I'm sure your mom and dad will be proud of you when I tell them how hard you worked."

"We loved working with you, Uncle Rudi. You are always so nice to us. And thanks for letting us stay with Aunt Klara. We feel much safer here than in Essen," said Hektor. Albert agreed.

Mother Nature did her job well. The cherries became churning pools of fermentation, and the odor of rotting fruit turning into alcohol was rising from one of the dank cisterns below the old house. Uncle Rudi was certain the fermenting process had reached its peak. The barrels were sealed before he departed for the hospital. Getting on the early train, he was confident the base for a high-quality product was once again resting in his cellars.

Three days after Uncle Rudi's departure, Aunt Klara and the boys were shaken by a loud and shattering explosion during the night.

The beds rocked and seemed to have been moved by the impact. Aunt Klara stormed into Albert and Hektor's bedroom.

"What was that?" she exclaimed.

"Do you think the village was bombed?" Hektor inquired.

"If it was, one of the bombs must have struck our house," Albert added.

Aunt Klara lit a candle, and they descended the steps with caution. All seemed to be OK so far. The kitchen was undisturbed. They finally dared to turn on lights in the inn; they didn't want to cause a gas explosion. All was intact. There wasn't any evidence of an attack on the building. The courtyard showed no signs of damage by bombs or incendiary devices. It couldn't have been lightning; it was a starry and clear night. They were puzzled.

"Let's open a kitchen window. Maybe the Böhms heard the explosion." Norbert peered out of his bedroom.

"Are you folks OK? I was awakened by a loud noise. Nothing wrong here. Did you hear the noise?"

"Not only did we hear it but we felt it since the beds appeared to have moved right off the floor," Aunt Klara replied.

"I'll come over and help you check the house." All was in order as he retraced their steps. In the courtyard, he saw another possibility.

"Let me open this clapboard door to the cistern." Norbert held up his lantern toward the whitewashed ceiling.

"I think we discovered the culprit. Look—you'll see what I mean."

They raised their eyes and followed the beam of his lantern. Everything was covered in muddy-red slime and little bumps. They discovered that one of the large barrels had exploded—that is, the trapdoor had been blown out. The smell was awful. The boys could not wait to get out of the cellar.

"What are we going to do about it?" they asked Aunt Klara and Norbert.

"Right now, I'm not sure. I will give Uncle Rudi a call in the morning and see if he confirms my suspicions." Rudi was surprised by the news.

"That must have been some bang! Was there any damage to the house that you can see?"

"None other than your wonderful cherries plastered all over the entire cellar. What do you want us to do about it?"

"I hate to tell you, but you and the boys have a major job ahead of you. Use dustpans or anything with a wide scoop to scrape the residue of the cherries off anything in sight. Simply take the scrapings and put them back into the barrel from which they emerged. From what you tell me, the only thing that was blown out was the large trapdoor on one of the barrels, right?"

"Yes, Rudi, that's all that seems to have happened. Norbert inspected the barrel, and it looked just fine. The mess it made is another story." She enlightened the boys as to the task at hand. It was a nightmarish ordeal.

"How can Uncle Rudi use this stuff with all the dirt and grime on the ceiling and floor mixed in?" asked Hektor.

"Oh, he assured me there was no harm in doing so. The fermentation process will continue, and all impurities will eventually settle on the bottom of the barrel. The distilling process will take care of the rest."

They scraped and collected mushy cherries and pits for days on end. Uncle Rudi would seal the renegade barrel during his next visit.

The "lazy" days of summer were almost gone; soon it was time to think about school. Both boys couldn't wait to do the Heil Hitler bit for Herr Lehrer Herb [Herr Teacher Herb].

On the last Thursday before their vacation ended, they all slept in after a hard day's work at the gardens in Heimbach. It was daylight. The house was completely still. The quiet was almost eerie. And then it happened. This time there wasn't a bang. The beds were rocking again. The wardrobe was moving as well. Pictures on the walls were swinging back and forth, as was the lamp hanging in the center of the ceiling. It was almost like the walls were moving themselves. The whole episode took only seconds—yet the impact seemed to last for an eternity.

Aunt Klara was shocked. *It could not have been a repeat of the cherry event; but what was it?*

"Boys, are you OK? Did you feel that? Did you notice the walls moving? Did you hear anything?"

"No, we heard nothing, but we were awakened by our moving beds and saw all that motion everywhere. The silence was almost deafening. We've never experienced anything like it."

"Neither have I! I turned on my old radio. Perhaps a distant city was bombed."

Within the hour, they had their answer. An earthquake occurred in the Vosges Mountains of Alsace-Lorraine. They were separated from this region by miles and the Rhine. The jolt was strong enough to frighten everyone.

"I'm glad it wasn't anything right here in the village. Boys, I'm off to Emmendingen to get my hair done. You can read or play some games. You don't have to do any jobs today after you worked so hard yesterday in my yard. Hopefully not all good things happen in threes."

"You must be kidding, Aunt Klara. 'Rock-a-my-bed' is an event we don't care to experience for a third time; twice in the course of our first summer in Köndringen is more than enough," said both boys, speaking in a singular voice.

〤

A couple weeks later, Hektor was happy to let his mother know that all her precious belongings had arrived and were safely tucked away at the Lion Inn. Everything found its place as Helena had envisioned and was now kept under lock and key. Aunt Klara offered to let them peek into the room, giving the boys a way of staying in touch with familiar items from their home. Hektor was glad to learn that his mother had kept her copy of *Gone with the Wind* in Essen. He knew how she enjoyed rereading certain passages.

When Helena wrote to them of the latest serious bombings, all were glad to know that the new bomb shelter had finally been finished. This gave Helena and her neighbors much-needed and improved protection. The bombings of target cities significantly increased. Köndringen remained unscathed. They stayed in touch with the world by hearing from family and friends. The news in papers and on the radio was filtered or controlled by the government.

Chapter 9

SUMMER was just about gone. The last grapes were harvested to become the treasured *Spätlese*. Abundant bales of hay were stored in barns. Busy hands of many women freed ears of corn from their husks and then tied the ears together in pairs. Strung on wires to dry, the kernels would feed fowl and hogs; dried husks were braided on long winter nights. They became uppers for house shoes and slippers that were lined with old corduroy from discarded shirts and pants. Soles were cut from retired bicycle tires and fit and glued to the soles of the slippers. Nothing was ever wasted. The storks congregated, saying farewell before flying to Africa with their 1943 offspring.

Hektor and Albert were enjoying their ten-day *Kartoffelferien* [potato vacation] in mid-October. Aunt Klara sent the boys on a last trek to Heimbach. She had concluded a bartering agreement with Herr Lang, the farmer bordering her property. He traded a handsome male goat for three bottles of Rudi's delectable Kirschwasser.

Off were Hektor and Albert to Heimbach. There was no need to rush. Soon they reached the Lang *Bauernhof* [homestead].

"Good day, boys. I gather you are here to fetch the goat for Frau Müller."

"Yes," said Albert. "Which one is it?"

"Oh, it's that big one over there. He is the one with the black ears and the big horns. He is quite spirited. I hope you two can get along with him. At times he can be stubborn and has a mind of his own." Hektor looked at Albert and then at Herr Lang.

"Are you sure we can do this? He looks like he is full of it."

"Let me show you how to handle him. This rope will help. If he doesn't behave, just give him a good yank. That will do the job. One of you can hold him by the rope. Hektor, you can use this willow cane to keep him moving. Tell Frau Müller I will stop by the Lion to pick up the Kirschwasser when I'm in town next week. Now, you best be off and on your way. It may take you a little longer with the goat in tow."

The trio walked out to the country lane. Using the left side of the road was a good idea. It allowed the boys to see the oncoming traffic of mostly oxen-drawn carts and now and then a motorcycle. The animal was on his best behavior. Suddenly Hektor piped up with a real brainstorm.

"Since he is marching along so nicely, what would you think of the idea of taking turns riding him?"

Albert thought for a moment and agreed. "That might be fun. We could pretend to be Jesus entering Jerusalem. Can you imagine what our friends will say when they see us sitting on top of a goat, riding through town? I can't wait to try it. And listen, I want to be the one who rides him into town—after all, I am the older one."

Hektor agreed—what else could he do? Albert pulled the goat off the road and made him stand next to a sizable boulder.

"OK, Hektor, climb up on that rock. I am holding him steady. Get your ass on the critter and hold on to both horns for dear life. You'll be just fine."

Hektor got on the goat before the critter made his first attempt at bucking him. Mr. Goat calmed down in response to the yanking and whipping. At last Hektor was riding high on the goat.

Some of the farmers passing them couldn't help but snicker.

They saw many things done by kids, but no one could recall seeing them ride a goat. That would make a good story to share over a beer at the Lion. The city slickers living with Klara Müller had become the talk of the town.

Closer to the village, they saw a huge plume of black smoke rising from a building somewhere near the church or the center of town.

"What is that?" cried Hektor.

"Looks like one big barn fire to me," replied Albert.

"I think it is actually very close to the inn. For all we know, the Gasthaus Lion is on fire."

"You are joking, aren't you? Can you just imagine all of Mom's things going up in smoke?"

"I don't even want to think about that, but I'm not joking! It could very well be the old inn."

They picked up their pace. They switched places riding the goat, with Albert manipulating the rope as well as the willow cane.

"Look, that goat is limping. You are too heavy for him!" yelled Hektor.

"Never mind, I still want to ride him into town."

Women were running toward town. Church bells were ringing incessantly. Fire alarms were blaring all over the countryside, summoning every available fire truck from adjacent villages and towns.

Closer in, they were happy to see that it wasn't the Lion that was burning. It was Pfitzer's detached new barn. No one was paying any attention to the high rider on the goat.

"Shucks! I hate to be upstaged by a fire!" Albert said. Klara spotted them as they turned into the alley.

"What on earth possessed you to ride the poor creature? No wonder it took you forever to get back. I was beginning to get worried about you two. I guess I'll hear about this from my patrons in the weeks to come. You two sure know how to call attention to yourselves. Get the critter in the courtyard, and close the gate tightly. The Lion is closed. Stay out of the way of the firemen." With the other kids, they perched on the steps of the inn to give them a perfect, straight-on view of the huge fire.

"Where are the Pfitzer kids? Does anyone know how the fire started?" Albert wanted to know. Udo, another loudmouth among the kids, turned to Albert.

"I'll tell you who did it, since you are obviously not smart enough to figure it out for yourself. It was Kurt and Irmgard. They went into the barn and smoked under the hay wagon stashed in the back. You know how much hay was stacked in the loft above them, don't you? Well, the hay on the ground caught on fire when they dropped one of their matches. They got scared shitless and ran and quietly closed the barn door behind them."

"Why didn't they call for help? I can't believe anyone is that stupid."

"Well, we can't all be as smart as you city slickers. They were just scared kids and didn't dare tell a soul what was happening."

Udo was shaking his head. "Riding a goat?" He snickered. "You've got to be kidding!" Aunt Klara finished the story.

"The hay apparently smoldered for quite a while. And then the gases from the ignited hay caused a huge explosion and blew the roof right off the top of the barn. With all that oxygen suddenly getting to the smoldering stuff, it turned instantly into an inferno. By the time all the fire and water trucks got here, the whole building was ablaze." Albert looked past Aunt Klara and addressed Udo.

"Thanks for letting me know—and more than I asked for, you smart-ass!" he yelled. Albert was ready to give Udo a fat lip.

The main attraction for the afternoon fizzled. Stomachs were growling since it was high time for their evening meal. Aunt Klara opened the doors to the Lion. Some patrons might have wanted to wash down the smoke and dust with a cold beer. A big guy sauntered into the pub in his dirty farming clothes.

"Draw me a cold beer." He saw Hektor and Albert through the kitchen door.

"Hey, guys, come here. You were quite a sight on the road from Heimbach. If you were riding an ass, I might have thought you were pretending to be Jesus entering Jerusalem." Little did he know, ass or no ass, the thought had crossed their minds.

✕

The boys planned to see their father late in the fall. Helena was concerned about their travels by train during daylight hours. Lately, trains were frequently attacked by low-flying planes, and many people had been killed.

On October 31, Hektor and Albert got on the five thirty train in Emmendingen and arrived in Baden-Baden shortly after seven o'clock. They had left in total darkness and arrived at their destination before daybreak. As their mother had told them, they got on the streetcar right in front of the railway station. Ten minutes later, they were at the Badischer Hof hospital.

"Goodness, you made great time. We didn't think you would be here any earlier than nine o'clock," said Uncle Rudi. They shook hands and gave their father a quick hug.

"Norbert took us to Emmendingen with his motorcycle—the one with the sidecar. It was one nifty ride. Albert sat behind Norbert, and I was in the sidecar. That way we were able to catch a fast train and didn't have to change."

"Our breakfast hasn't even been brought. Maybe you boys will be lucky, and one of the good sisters will feed you as well."

With that, Sister Angelika swept into the room, carrying the breakfast trays for Alex and Rudi. Hektor snickered when he beheld that headpiece on the nun. She was young, very beautiful, and looked stunning in her cloister regalia. Talk about making an entrance.

"What a nice surprise to see these young men. Are these your sons, Herr Birken? Boys, I like those nice suits you are wearing. You are regular fashion plates."

"My wife bought those suits for the boys here in Baden-Baden, when she was visiting a few weeks ago." He didn't mention the tongue-lashing he got at the time—and certainly not what had provoked Helena's anger.

"Yes, this is Albert, my older son, and his younger brother, Hektor. Maybe you haven't heard. They are staying with Herr Müller's wife in Köndringen, a good hour south of here. The Müllers came to our rescue. The boys had to get out of Essen. They are having a great time in the little village." He motioned to the good sister to bend down to him. When the boys were horsing around with Rudi, he turned close to the sister's ear.

"By the way, what happened to nurse Carlotta? We haven't seen her in a week." Sister Angelika whispered in Alex's ear.

"She was fired. They found her in bed with one of you soldiers." She almost knocked off her headgear as she straightened to stand up. Both boys giggled. Alex was glad it wasn't he who got caught. That affair clearly was over.

"Well, have you boys had your breakfast? You must have gotten up pretty early to be here at this hour. I'm sure I can find something that will be to your liking."

"We did get up shortly after four. Aunt Klara warmed some oatmeal she made last night. It was good. We didn't leave on empty stomachs. We could eat some breakfast with Father and Uncle Rudi, though, right, Hektor?"

"Yes, we surely could. Thank you for being so nice to us, Sister Angelika."

"Uncle Rudi and I will get started on our breakfast before it gets cold. We can talk a little in between bites until Sister brings your breakfast. I have a surprise for you. You are going home over the Christmas holidays. It's a special request of your Godmother, Aunt Georgine. She has finally resolved to marry Franz Dimmelsburg and insists that you boys be there for the event. What do you say now?"

"How will we get there?"

"Your mother and I believe you are experienced travelers at this point. After that solo journey to Köndringen and trips you made to see me, we feel confident that you can do it on your own. There is one more surprise. Aunt Elsa will bring you back here and stay with you for a few weeks. She closed her store and has nothing better to do. Won't that be fun?"

"Sure!" the boys said in one voice. They always had a good time with their two aunts. They were still smiling from ear to ear when Sister Angelika made her second grand entrance, this time with breakfast. It looked pretty sumptuous.

In early October, both boys started to break out with all sorts of boils from head to toe. Aunt Klara had them checked at the hospital in Emmendingen. The doctors informed her that both Albert and Hektor suffered from blood poisoning, most likely caused by eating unwashed fruit that had been sprayed with chemicals.

Since they both looked like undesirable outcasts, they felt it was best to let their mother know ahead of time. They warned her in one of their rare telephone conversations. This way she wouldn't have the shock of her life.

"Mom, don't faint when you greet us at the train. Both Hektor and I are covered with boils everywhere. The doctors in Emmendingen told Aunt Klara we have blood poisoning from eating unwashed fruit. It will take some time before we heal completely. Aunt Klara says we look like lepers, whatever that means."

"Glad for the warning. We'll deal with it when you get home. In the meantime, I will confer with my trusted homeopath. Look forward to seeing you. Love you!" And she was gone.

On December 19, the boys embarked on their journey. The trip was uneventful, and they were looking forward to seeing their mother. Helena was waiting for the arrival of the express train from Cologne. She had last seen the boys in summer. As they got off, she couldn't hide her tears.

"My God, how you have grown. Albert, you are taller than I. And, Hektor, you look like a beanpole. You must have had a real growth spurt. I know you are fed well, but you are skin and bones."

Albert having surpassed her height was no big deal; Mother Birken was tiny – not even five feet tall. Hektor's appearance, as always, put fear into her heart.

"I'm glad I was forewarned about your boils. At least your faces don't look worse right now."

"Wait until you see our arms and legs!"

"I can't wait!"

Hektor and Albert carried their suitcases themselves as they made their way quickly to the car. This was a new experience. They were not so certain about getting into a car driven by their mother. Actually, she did just fine, and they were impressed by the competence of her maneuvers in traffic. There were not many other civilian vehicles, but she had to get around buses, streetcars, and trucks.

"Wow, Mom, you are doing well driving that bug of yours through city traffic. You've become a confidant driver!" volunteered Albert. Hektor wasn't so sure. He firmly held on to one of the braces; he could feel the perspiration in his armpits.

The dark of the night hid many ugly sights, and Hektor and Albert were not aware of much of the destruction already visited upon their hometown. Their house was still standing sturdily amid many burnt-out shells, although it was badly pockmarked by shrapnel. The vacant look of holes where once were windows and doors gave all the houses a ghostly appearance in the bright moonlight that evening.

"What happened to Pfeiffer's house, and to Fillipusis's?" asked Albert.

"They were bombed and burned to the ground. Those houses didn't have a chance without concrete ceilings and walls. The stairways were old and wooden, and carried the flames rapidly from one floor to the next. All those neighbors are gone. You will find there are no other children in the area. They, like you, were all sent away." The kids had not even thought about this when they embarked on their visit. They didn't expect their own home to look so primitive.

"Mom, how can you live without any furniture? These crates and cartons look terrible. What gives with the potbelly contraption in the middle of the living room? When did you get it? How can you cook and bake with that thing for the three of us?" Helena gave the boys a not-so-convincing rundown of her wartime menus.

"Most of the time I make brown soup. It takes some browned, almost-burnt flour thinned with water and some seasoning. I don't bake cakes for myself. I can make a doughlike mixture and cook the cake in a boiling-water bath. The cake will have no color; maybe a chocolate-like glaze might make it more appealing for you kids.

"If and when I cook meat, potatoes, and a vegetable, I prepare them in this series of stacked pots. The thing that takes the longest I cook first. Then the pots are stacked one on top of the other to keep everything warm until we can eat. When all is ready, I start heating the water to wash our dishes."

The boys thought things were primitive in Köndringen. They had no idea how their mother lived these days. They checked out their bedroom. The outside walls were actually covered with ice. The wallpaper was peeling off. Carpets were nailed to the frames where once there were windows.

"Isn't that the rug that used to lie in front of our beds?" asked Albert.

"Yes. And look at this. The bathroom door became your bedstead under the old mattress."

"Man, things are pretty bad."

Blankets and bedspreads had taken the place of doors. The featherbeds were still there; there was no way they could sleep without them.

"Mutti, this looks pretty grim. We thought things were primitive in Aunt Klara's old house."

"If you thought cooking is a challenge, wait until the three of us take a bath. I take mine in a wooden tub close to the potbelly stove. It's easier than carrying the hot water to the bathroom. Also, there is a little more warmth in the living room. Yes, boys, times have changed."

Hektor and Albert were happy to learn Grandma and Grandpa Krämer's modern house had survived all the bombings. At this point, nothing had been sent to a safer location. Aunt Georgine's wedding was to be at her parents' home.

Everyone in the family had hoarded their ration stamps, especially for meat, eggs, and butter. Helena could be of some help. Grandpa Krämer collected on favors due.

Christmas Eve was disappointing, with a few homemade presents under the sickly looking tree. It was a real tree, all right. There were no decorations. Hektor and Albert cut out a dove from a piece of white cardboard and adorned the top of the tree. Used advent candles made up the rest of the Christmas décor. This was clearly an occasion to be forgotten. A humble meal was shared with the Jokkish couple who lived directly above the Birken apartment and business. Julius Jokkish had become the sole man in the building and often stood side by side with Helena.

Christmas Day was spent with the grandparents. The meal was a marked improvement. Much of the day was consumed with preparations for Aunt Georgine's wedding.

Georgine and Franz had their civil service at the city hall on the last working day before Christmas. As far as Aunt Georgine was concerned, that did the trick. She was not a particularly religious person. But to appease her mother and Helena, she agreed for the neighborhood pastor to perform a brief service in her parents' living room.

"Helena, I hope you are happy. I just don't give a hoot about all this folderol and the church. How can you still believe in any of that stuff with the things that are happening all around us?"

Helena touched her eyes with a lacy handkerchief. She didn't have a ready answer. Conveniently for Georgine, the Evangelical Church in the district had been destroyed earlier in the month. To Georgine, the bombed-out church was a blessing in disguise.

The pastor's service was over in a flash, which was OK with the boys. Some of the minister's sermons were tedious and boring. The village pastor in Köndringen was not too bad; at least he wasn't so long-winded.

Grandma Krämer pulled out all the stops. The big ebony dining room table was set with her very best Rosenthal china and fine crystal. She used her finest cutwork linen and napkins that she lovingly had stitched as a young girl. None of them would see such opulence in family circles again until well after the war.

For now, all, including the minister and his wife, looked forward to a decent, warm meal. Pork and mutton were prepared and served as elegantly as a roast beef or filet mignon might have been at another time. Helena unobtrusively pinched her nose; she covered her face with a dainty handkerchief when they brought out the mutton, which she positively detested. If it hadn't been her sister's wedding meal, she would have made a spectacle of herself. As bad as things became, she simply could not tolerate the odor and taste of mutton. Helena would rather have had brown soup. Instead, she politely declined and held her breath as the platter was passed in front of her. She sampled the pork, red cabbage, and mashed potatoes, as did the boys.

The next day Aunt Georgine and Uncle Franz left on their *Flitterwochen* [honeymoon]. Hektor and Albert thought that to be a funny word, "flitter" having the connotation of busily flapping one's wings like a hummingbird. They envisioned Aunt Georgine and Uncle Franz flittering around each other. Somehow neither struck them as the flittering type. The Dimmelsburgs were headed south and eventually would spend a few days in Baden-Baden. Franz was quite the gambler and was looking forward to making a killing at the casino.

New Year's Eve had been another bust. In prewar years, their father liked to shoot off lots of firecrackers. No such displays were allowed during wartime.

Hektor suffered from postholiday depression. *Why does it have to go by so fast? Now we have to wait for another year until Christmas rolls around again.* However, both boys were looking forward to their return to Köndringen, especially since Aunt Elsa would accompany them.

Tearful goodbyes were exchanged, and the train hurried them toward their little village in Baden. Aunt Elsa planned to visit Alex her first weekend in Köndringen. She was anxious to see him. Alex; her husband, Ferdinand; and her brother, Arthur, were the only family members not present at the gathering in Essen. Aunt Elsa wanted the boys to have a great time while visiting their dad in Baden-Baden.

The first night at the resort, Aunt Elsa and the boys joined Aunt Georgine and Uncle Franz for dinner. The meal was elegantly served, although the food was not anything to brag about. They arrived at the casino.

"Sorry, sir, children are not allowed in the casino!" They were stopped by a uniformed doorman.

"We are on our honeymoon. Our nephews have been separated from their parents for the duration of the war. Their dad lies in the Badischer Hof. We want to show them a good time. How about looking the other way?" Uncle Franz stuck a fifty-mark bill in the guy's hand. He let all of them pass.

The casino was buzzing with elegantly dressed women and

civilian men in dark attire, often tuxedos. The soldiers wore much fancier uniforms with more ribbons, medals, and war decorations dripping from their chests than the boys had ever seen on their father or Uncle Rudi. Hektor could not take his eyes off one of the officers. The guy was strutting around like a peacock. He had a piece of glass or a lens attached to a black string stuck in his right eye—that is, he was trying to keep it stuck in the eye socket. It constantly fell out, much to the gentleman's chagrin. Every time it popped out, he quickly tucked it in again. Hektor quietly turned to his uncle.

"Uncle Franz, what is that thing that officer is trying to keep stuck in his eye socket?"

"That's called a monocle. Some men are so vain they don't want to wear eyeglasses. Sometimes they wear it strictly for effect. I think that gentleman is wearing it to impress people." Hektor had to turn his head. He would have laughed into the man's face; he thought it was that funny.

Uncle Franz gave his entourage the high sign to follow him to one of the gambling tables. He and Aunt Georgine knew what to do; Aunt Elsa and the boys stood back and watched them play at the roulette table. The boys were intrigued by all the French phrases repeatedly fired at the players by the croupier. The boys didn't understand what all the hollering was about, but they noticed how large sums of money quickly changed hands. It was all so exciting! Everyone had a great time. Hektor forgot how sad he was that the holidays and the family reunion had passed by so quickly. He thought the epilogue in Baden-Baden was far more fun and exciting than "the gathering" in Essen.

Elsa and the boys were pleased to see Alex was not flat on his back when they visited him; it was the first time for the boys to see their father trying to stand on his feet since they came to see him during the last year. The sisters were teaching him to walk with crutches. He had a few close calls but eventually seemed to get the hang of things. The nuns were working their hardest to get him walking. He had been lying in bed far too long. In that respect, Uncle Rudi was doing much better. Although he was still limping, he could get around easily just using a cane.

Chapter 10

ALEX made a call to Helena in early September 1944. It was relatively late for Helena, since she was still leaving for the markets very early in the morning.

"Why are you calling me—and at this hour?" Helena posed with considerable annoyance in her voice.

"I am being discharged from the hospital. Can you meet me at the train station? I'm coming home on crutches."

"I know it won't be easy for you. But, before you come home, I want you to take a train to Köndringen and pick up the boys!"

"Why would I want to do that? They are much better off where they are!"

"Never mind. Just get yourself on the train. We'll talk about it when you are here!" Helena could tell Alex had no idea what was going on.

"You know there is only one train running between Karlsruhe and Dortmund, don't you, Alex? It's supposed to arrive in Essen at six o'clock in the evening. Be prepared to be late, since daytime trains are often attacked by *Tiefflieger* [low-flying planes]. Don't even attempt to get off the train. You, being on crutches, will never make it. Just flop your body on the floor of the compartment when the passengers are told to flee from the train. And don't get up until they give the all clear. You may need someone to help you up."

What the hell is she talking about? Alex looked startled.

She hung up. He could tell Helena was utterly disgusted.

Her mind was racing. She needed a plan of attack in dealing with this latest debacle. Because of the total blackout, it was pitch dark when she walked a couple blocks down the street to speak with her friend Mimi.

Mimi Foster operated a fruit and vegetable stand. They'd met at the wholesale market two years earlier. Helena knocked on Mimi's makeshift door. She was surprised to see her.

"Sorry if I managed to get you up at this hour of the night. Alex is being discharged from the hospital tomorrow. Would you mind driving me in the Steyr to the Bahnhof? He is supposed to arrive about six in the evening; I'm catching a train an hour later toward Köndringen to fetch the boys since Alex refused to get them. Of course, he has no clue what's happening. I didn't dare say any more on the phone. I'm sure my phone has been monitored for a long time. Often when I pick up the phone, I hear strange noises in the background."

Mimi interrupted her. "You want to come in for a few moments? Would you care for a drink?"

"I sure could use one. I know I'm not supposed to drive the car for private and personal pleasure. I assume using it to transport an injured soldier might be as good an excuse as any. Sorry to bother you tonight, but I knew you wouldn't be home first thing in the morning. And you know me—I need to have a plan." Mimi winked at Helena. Her offering of a drink had been her attempt at slowing down Helena's river of words.

"Of course I'll help you, although you realize what a challenge it is for me to squeeze my giant body into that little bug of yours." Mimi was tall and weighed well over one hundred kilos. Helena was just a little mite and very trim. She used to say, *Klein aber o-ho* [little, but watch out]! Mimi touched her right index finger to her lips.

"Be careful when you speak! Keep your voice down. The blankets aren't a good sound barrier. I've become so intimidated since they picked up Rachel a few weeks ago. Every time I think about it, I can still see those blackguards dragging her mercilessly out of the house and dumping her into the back of that truck. I told you they shipped her off to Theresienstadt, didn't I?" Helena shuddered.

"I often questioned how long it would be before they would take her. It was the need for her professional services and being married to a Christian that protected her from being nabbed."

Helena turned Theresienstadt over in her mind. That was supposed to be the concentration camp not far from Prague. She wondered what the war criminals had done to her dear friend.

Ж

Helena and Mimi met Alex at the train station. He was about thirty minutes late. Helena gave Alex a quick hug as he hobbled off the train with his crutches. One could tell she wasn't greeting her long-lost love. She grabbed the little suitcase a porter was carrying for him and handed it to Mimi. She slapped a couple of marks into the porter's hand and trained her eyes on Alex and spouted.

"By the way, this is Mimi Foster, my friend, who will drive you home and make sure you get into the house. You probably won't recognize the business, with the store windows bricked in and other doors and windows covered up in cardboard, blankets, rugs, and bedspreads. You'll get used to it. I have to run to the other platform to catch my train to Karlsruhe."

"What are you talking about!" yelled Alex. Helena was already thirty feet away. She was running to catch her train south.

"I'll fill you in on our way home," interrupted Mimi. She had heard of his choleric outbursts and tantrums.

Armed with her little overnight satchel, Helena caught all her connections. She enjoyed the relatively comfortable ride on the overnight train. She arrived in Köndringen on the morning of September 13. When she got to the gates of the Lion, no one was more shocked than Klara and her charges. Helena's face was flushed. She was blowing air like a whale. She had moved her little feet just a bit too quickly. Helena was anxious to see her boys and Klara. All of them knew how impulsive and explosive she could be. Her appearance was a total surprise.

Mother Birken had caught some much-needed sleep on the Astral Express from Cologne to Karlsruhe; she was not missing a beat. The all-nighter was a blessing. Trains traveling under the cloak of darkness were much less vulnerable to attacks.

"Klara, I'm here to take the boys and a few of my things home," she announced, having barely greeted Klara and her sons.

"Helena, I thought Alex was determined to leave Hektor and Albert with me for the duration of the war. What made him change his mind?"

"He didn't change his; neither did I change mine. I could not explain to him on the phone why I want us to be together in Essen at this moment. He has no idea what's happening with the war. I have a pretty good one from listening to BBC broadcasts on my well-hidden shortwave radio. Luckily, it functions on battery power. I take every opportunity to hear what's happening. Of course, I have to be extremely circumspect when and where I do my listening. With doors and windows mostly gone, it isn't easy to be private."

"Slow down, Helena. You are talking too fast. I still don't understand why you want to take the boys back to Essen now."

"This damn war isn't going to last much longer. When the end comes, there will be no way for us to communicate with you by phone, mail, or even in person. Roads and railroads will be nonexistent in the end. If we are meant to survive this nightmare, we will survive it together. If not, we will perish together. The Nazis are right when they draw parallels between the civil war in the States and the present disaster. They call World War II the second *totaler Krieg* [total war]. There may be few survivors. Who would want to leave their children alone, surviving such chaos?" Klara had to agree with Helena's assessment. Hektor and Albert had no choice.

"Go upstairs to your room and start packing your things. Take all your clothes and shoes. Remember, there is nothing left in Essen. Furthermore, there won't be anything new to buy. What you have here will have to do until the bloody end." Albert stared at his mother.

"Why are you taking us back to Essen when you know there will be more bombings? We didn't even know there was a war as long as we were here. Hektor is scared out of his mind to go back home. What are you thinking, Mother?"

"Don't question my decision to take you home. As I told Aunt Klara, this war will not last very much longer. When it is over, we will not be able to get in touch with anyone in the country. You won't know what happened to us, and we will not be able to learn what happened to you. I know it's a terrible thing to say to someone as young as you boys, but either we shall survive this nightmare together or we'll all die together." Albert and Hektor stood there not believing what their mother had just told them.

"I will go to the room with our belongings and look for a few practical things for myself; fancy dresses I don't need. My heavy skirts might come in handy."

She moved the hangers in the wardrobe and selected sturdy skirts and jackets. Anything dressy she then packed in a large carton Klara gave her.

"I am taking nothing for your father. Suits he can't wear; the last thing he sputtered about was to leave his good uniforms in safety. Lord knows why. If I have anything to say about it, he will never wear another one."

Klara realized that any attempts at changing Helena's mind

were futile. She retreated to the kitchen and fixed a hearty breakfast. What Helena could have used was a spot of Rudi's Kirschwasser. She might have imbibed had it not been much too early in the day for her to do so in front of the kids. When Helena and her boys descended to the pub, the large round table in the far northeast corner was set. Helena enjoyed the hearty homemade bread carved in rather thick, manly slices.

"Nothing dainty about this meal," she said.

There were coarse liverwurst, preserved in a can, and a variety of cheeses. Margarine had to do. Klara had some decent mustard that added a little moisture to the open-faced sandwiches all of which were prepared on their little wooden eating boards. Quietly, they ate their last meal at the Lion. Finally, Helena spoke up.

"You are all acting as if it were your *Henker's Mahlzeit* [a prisoner's last meal before execution]." That's how they felt. Klara was convinced Helena and her loved ones were heading into troubled waters.

Of course, Klara had no idea what the end of the war held in store for her. Rudi had been discharged a few days earlier than Alex. He had twenty-four hours before starting his hasty departure for the eastern front. Klara's days would be busy, but she would miss her boys. She had learned to love them like a mother; Hektor and Albert loved her in return.

Klara arranged for Norbert to take Helena and the boys as well as herself to the train station. There were a few more things to carry than when Hektor and Albert arrived. Helena's trousseau trunk was checked through to Essen as soon as she had finished packing. Norbert had been kind enough to drop it off with the stationmaster. On this chilly morning, the boys sat with Norbert on top of the horse-drawn carriage. Klara and Helena sat in a huddle in the back with the luggage. They didn't mind. It gave them a chance to say their quiet goodbyes; they cried and shared their misery without being observed.

The local train pulled into the depot. Smaller bags were carried by the travelers rushing onto the train. Norbert handed bigger pieces of luggage through the open window to save time. The red cap raised his signal for the engineer and blew his whistle. The engine replied with gusto as it repeatedly spit out gusts of blackened steam setting the train in motion. Helena, Hektor, and Albert hung out of the open window, waving their handkerchiefs wildly, underscoring their farewell. It was goodbye to a chapter in their lives the boys would ultimately regard as the happiest of their childhoods.

Helena counted her blessings. She and the boys were alone in the compartment for now. Not knowing who was next to them or how soundproof trains were these days, she started speaking quietly. She bent down and put her arms around both boys.

"There are some things I need to tell you. If you think things were bad when you were home eight months ago, you better be prepared for the worst. There is no running water, electricity, or gas. Streetcars and buses hardly run anymore. I can no longer use the streetcars to get to your grandparents. Many streets are torn up or badly damaged; but worse, I no longer dare drive my car for personal use. When we visit Grandma and Grandpa, we must walk. There may come a time when you will have to help me do certain things for your grandparents. They are getting older and need my assistance. We will talk about this later." Hektor and Albert were all ears. It sounded like the easy life of yesterday was over.

"You remember Ulrike, the girl who worked with me in the store, don't you? She's gone," Helena practically whispered into their ears. "Once the streetcars stopped running, the walk from across town became too much for her. And guess what? As soon as she applied for some kind of unemployment compensation, they nabbed her."

"Mutti, what do you mean by they 'nabbed her?' Did they put her in jail?"

"Oh no! She was put in a uniform and sent off to the eastern front. She always blabbered about wanting to die for her *Führer*. Maybe unwittingly she made that opportunity possible. You know I could not fire her. I had to be so careful with her around. Had she ever discovered my hidden radio, they would have arrested me a long time ago. Ulrike would not have hesitated for even a second to report me to the authorities. I'm glad she is no longer with us." Albert kept asking more questions.

"But if Ulrike is gone, who is running the store while you came to get us? Dad wouldn't know what or how to do it. I assume he is still walking with crutches?"

"Oh yes, a friend of mine drove him home. I had no other choice but to close for a couple of days. And you are right—your father is there, but he is useless and can't run the store. I almost wish they hadn't sent him home. Now I have to worry about him and you boys. Things were a lot easier when I just needed to worry about myself."

"Then why the heck didn't you leave us in Köndringen? We were perfectly happy staying with Aunt Klara. You make it sound like we are not really welcome in our own home."

"Sorry, Albert, I didn't mean to say that. I just have a lot on my mind. Now I am truly the captain of our ship. You, your father, and I have to stick together—we are all we have."

Looking back, Hektor thought his mother had a great deal of trust in her young boys. So often kids were taken in and brainwashed by the authorities and did not think anything the worse for accidentally betraying their own parents. Luckily for Helena, that was not the case with Hektor and Albert.

Reaching Karlsruhe, they switched to the express train. Helena was fortunate to find a porter who was willing to help her with getting her luggage to the connecting train. Unfortunately, they also lost their privacy in the compartment. All seats had been taken by passengers. With a little luck, there would be no additional adult passengers entering the compartment. If there were, the boys might lose their seats.

Shortly after they laid claim to the space, Helena discovered their window did not close tightly. It hung crookedly in its frame. Open at the top by about four inches, it was jammed, and no one could close it. Helena took her coat and used it as a windbreak. That was a lot easier than taking chances at looking for a different compartment.

Early in the afternoon, when they were just outside of Wiesbaden, the train came to an abrupt halt. Someone had pulled the emergency brakes. They could hear the conductor yell as loud as he could with his megaphone.

"Everyone get off this train and lie as flat as possible in the nearest ditch. Wait until I blow my whistle again before you get back on. There are low-flying planes in the area. They will be shooting at the train and passengers. Whatever you do, stay as flat as you can make yourselves."

Helena and the boys sprinted as fast as their feet carried them and belly flopped into a ditch down from the train track. Bursts of gunfire punctuated the frightened utterances coming from the trench. The whole episode lasted only seconds. Soon the conductor blew his whistle, allowing the passengers to return to their seats. Some of the windows were shattered, but no one in their wagon was hurt. One of their suitcases had been struck by a large bullet. Luckily, there wasn't a fire—just a couple Helena's skirts were torn and had become "holy." The train was able to move on. They were lucky. Lately, other travelers along this route were not as fortunate. That bit of excitement was just a taste of things to come. They stepped out of the Hauptbahnhof.

"Mutti, I can't believe what I am seeing. This looks terrible! I can clearly see all the way to the synagogue—what's left of it," said Albert.

Helena was hoping their streetcar might be running again. It was one of the major arteries to neighboring towns. Luckily, there hadn't been any bombings in the couple of days she was gone. She turned to an older man standing near the platform.

"Have the tracks of the number eighteen been restored?"

"Yes, ma'am, number eighteen has been running again since yesterday afternoon."

Helena sighed; she was not so sure if she could have handled walking home. Mimi had told her on the phone that she had a good friend with a truck who would haul the trunk from the Hauptbahnhof to Kupferstrasse. The walk with the smaller luggage from the streetcar stop was long enough. Hektor and Albert each carried two pieces. They were all huffing and puffing when they arrived at Kupferstrasse. The building was even more pockmarked than the boys remembered. Their father greeted them.

"Welcome to the castle of rugs and blankets. Mother's brown soup is just about warm enough to eat."

Hektor and Albert thought it tasted awful, but at least it gave them something warm in their bellies. Their mother could not even begin to think about cooking anything else.

"Tomorrow would be another day." *Gone with the Wind* had become the family Bible. Loaned from friend to friend, it was always joyously welcomed home. Helena loved rereading some of her favorite passages by candlelight if necessary. She took every opportunity to emulate Scarlett O'Hara when it came to dealing with individuals in authority or predicaments that did not sit well with her.

Chapter 11

SEPTEMBER 23, 1944, was the night Hektor and Albert first experienced a major bombing since their return. They had forgotten what it was like to be under attack. The bunker was almost packed to capacity.

"Come here, boys, put your heads in my lap. Perhaps this heavy pillow will block out the sounds of the falling bombs," said their father.

Alex was holding the boys tightly. He could tell by their sweaty hands how frightened they were. Even with the pillow, they could hear the bombs traveling through the air, never knowing where they were going to strike.

"You don't hear the one that hits closest to you," Julius Jokkish said.

Some consolation that was. Hektor and Albert realized that evening that bombings were not exciting, but downright scary. They began to hate the whistling sound of falling bombs and the cacophony of crashing buildings that would follow each detonation.

They survived the attack. Standing in front of their house, they saw the orange light created by the inferno surrounding them. It was so bright they could have read a newspaper. Worst of all were the flames and the stench of burning flesh.

"There's that strange smell again," said one of the boys. Helena hustled them away.

The next attack came on October 11. The bombings occurred during daylight. The Allies discovered their bombs could be more closely pinpointed and have a more strategic effect. From that day on, many cities regularly experienced daytime bombings. When it was all over, Alex made a decision and spoke to his family.

"This is the last attack we spent in our bunker. I feel like a trapped animal. I'm scared shitless and know exactly how the boys must feel. I never had such fear when I was close to the front. I don't care what you say, Helena. The boys and I will not be in that shelter again."

"How do you expect to do that, Alex?"

"As soon as the first alarm goes off, we will run for the public bunker at Breslauerstrasse. If they warn us early enough, even I should make it. Being hundreds of feet underground, we shouldn't have to listen to those horrible sounds. If we make it to one of the entrances, we should be fairly safe."

What they listened to in the underground bunker were the frightened voices of those inside the shelter and the steady drip of water escaping from the concrete tunnel vaults above them. For once Helena agreed with Alex, and she knew what needed to be done.

"Sorry to tell you this, boys. From now on, you have to sleep in your clothes and shoes. You must always be ready to run to the bomb shelter. Your father and I have to do the same. It's not easy for any of us."

A couple nights later, they were running to the shelter when Hektor screamed as a large, bright ball of light fell out of the sky. Within seconds, the single ball multiplied rapidly into many smaller bright lights.

"*Vati*, look! There is a lighted Christmas tree in the sky. It almost seems like we are having a full moon."

"Hektor, the attackers are dropping that ball to make it easier to see where they want to drop their bombs. It ain't a Christmas tree. Stop looking at that thing and keep moving. The bombs will start falling any second now."

Winter of 1944–1945 was one of the coldest on record. Another lackluster Christmas had passed. What would the new year bring? Hektor went to the bomb shelter with his father to hear Hitler's message of hope. Helena and Albert couldn't care less. Hektor's mother knew what a worthless diatribe it would be. Near the main entrance was a heated hut. Mostly adults stood around all bundled in their warmest rags. The caretaker turned up the radio. At midnight Hitler began the shouting match in his inimitable fashion. What he said went over Hektor's head. Most of the adults weren't impressed either.

Later Hektor would recall the enormity of walking with his hobbling father over snow and ice. He remembered the clarity of the night, the sounds associated with the walk, and the indescribable beauty of the peaceful firmament above. Somehow the message from the "great leader" had little effect on the young boy.

Chapter 12

THE last major bombing of Essen occurred during daylight on March 11, 1945. It went on for hours. Helena and the boys were thankful they were deep underground. Alex was right. It would have been a nightmare in Helena's private bunker. The house on Kupferstrasse survived. The next morning Helena opted to take the boys to see their grandparents. It was a miserable long walk. Albert finally spoke up.

"Mother, why are you making us walk and see all this destruction?"

"I have to know what happened to your grandparents. They are old, and I need to look after them. Neither of my sisters nor my brother are here to help. And you have not seen them since Hektor's birthday in February. So don't make this anymore difficult for me than it is." When they walked down Rosalindenstrasse, they saw many destroyed houses.

"This does not look good. I'm frightened what we might see when we get closer."

Helena was right. As they approached the corner of the street, they could tell that only half of the house built in 1906 was still standing.

"Boys, we have to go on to Ratsherrnweg and see what happened to your grandparents' current home. It's a much newer house and might have withstood the attack." Hektor wanted to know how much further they had to walk after they battled damaged sidewalks and streets for almost two hours.

"Boys, we are almost there. I'm sorry to put you through this, but I must know if my parents survived this nightmare."

It didn't take much longer before they faced the totally demolished structure. A neighbor three houses down from her parents' home recognized Helena and the boys standing in front of the ruin.

"Hello, Frau Birken. All eighteen in the bomb shelter of the house were dug out. They are all alive, but your parents were not among them. We thought they might have been visiting you." Helena hugged her boys and started to cry.

"They must have been visiting my uncle and aunt, and I hope they were all spared. It's too far for us to walk. My boys and I are exhausted; it will take us hours to get back to our own home. Thank you for telling me that my parents were not among those who were in the house when it was struck."

She held on to the boys' hands and headed for the long walk home.

"What are you mumbling, Mutti?" asked Albert.

"I'm praying that your grandparents were with Uncle Gottlieb and Aunt Marla, and that all of them are safe. It will take days before we'll know for sure if they were spared."

A week later, Helena finally got word that her parents were alive. They had indeed been visiting the Reuters, whose home was miraculously not hit by bombs.

What saved the lives of the eighteen in the cellar of the Krämer villa was the foot-and-a-half-thick concrete ceiling reinforced with the oaken supports Franz Dimmelsburg had insisted on installing. Two bombs struck the house—one traveled through the stairway and the other hit the back of the building. The force lifted the house, popping out the walls and laying the three thick concrete ceilings one on top of the other like a stack of pancakes.

Essen lay in ruins. Its citizens faced the immensity of the total destruction. After the last attack, people could hear the constant noise of approaching artillery fire. The front was moving closer every day. The sound of tanks and cannons firing at each other became ever more pronounced.

The last week in March, Alex was minding the empty store. There was next to nothing to sell—even matches, toothpicks, and salt were rationed.

Hektor was in the little sitting room next to the store. He had an unobstructed view; the two-way mirror was broken long ago. Uncharacteristically, Albert had his nose in a book. Hektor watched his father standing with two canes behind the counter. Two Brownshirts entered and handed him a pink piece of paper. He rested the cane in his right hand against the counter and quickly read what had been handed to him. Immediately he called Helena.

"These gentlemen have something to tell you; you better speak to them yourself."

His sweaty hands clutched the canes more firmly. He was scared to death of the Nazis. When Helena appeared, she continued putting a clean cover on a bed pillow.

"Yes, what's this all about? To what do we owe the honor of your presence? I would have thought you already left for safer territory." Her face reflected biting sarcasm.

"Please read this document; it concerns you directly," demanded one of the Brownshirts.

Hektor and Albert were listening and watching more closely.

Their mother gave a cursory glance to the document Alex had set on the counter; it didn't take her long to discover what they were after. The slip of paper, supposedly an official government release, simply stated that her car, her precious Steyr, was requisitioned. She would be compensated for her contribution to the cause after the glorious victory of the German army.

Helena set the pillow and pillowcase on the counter. She took the pink slip and tore it into four pieces. She handed the scraps back to the closest of the uniformed men and glared, looking straight into his eyes.

"Glorious victory, my foot. I wouldn't consider wiping my ass with that worthless piece of paper. Where do you think I got that car? How do you think I paid for it? I worked for it! I didn't win it on some racetrack. You people thought you would conquer and rule the world. Now that you are at your rope's end, you want to confiscate private property and transport your useless fat bodies to safety with stolen property. Get out of here. I hope I never lay eyes again on another one of you damned gold pheasants."

She didn't miss a beat, but her face had turned red with rage. She turned around and left them and Alex standing in the empty store—speechless.

Once they clicked their heels and "Heil Hitlered" Alex in a farewell salute, he stumbled into the sitting room. Helena wasn't about to be intimidated.

"Why are you so scared of them? They are on the run. They know it, and I know it. No way are they going to take my car. Only over my dead body. Where did I put my screwdrivers?"

She remembered they were in one of the crates. Helena picked one that would do the job and headed for her Steyr. She opened the hood and deftly removed the distributor cap. She brought it into the house and put it in her giant purse.

"That thing goes with me everywhere. If they want it, they have to take me, too, or carry the car away!" And that was the end of it as far as she was concerned. She remained true to herself; she was gutsy right to the bitter end.

Afterward, they learned the two Nazis pulled the same stunt next door with the pharmacist, Bertold Gutz. He was taken in by their spiel and was dumb enough to fall for the trick. The Brown-shirts told him that Mrs. Birken was very fortunate. If things weren't what they were, they would make sure she would spend the remainder of her days in a concentration camp. They didn't use that term, but Herr Gutz knew what they were referring to. Indeed, Hektor's mother was fearless—but also very lucky.

1945–1948

Chapter 13

APRIL 11, 1945, marked the end of the war and a new beginning for Essen. A city of almost 650,000 counted less than half its citizens when Allied tanks rolled through the war-torn streets. While 32,000 deaths were certified, thousands of the city's souls were never accounted for.

The frenetic activities in the Birken household and business—whatever was left of it—climaxed on the day before they spotted the first American tank approaching their house. The copy of *Mein Kampf* and incriminating war photographs Alex had taken in Kiev were burned in the potbelly stove. The day Alex's regiment had marched up one of the major boulevards of Kiev, they encountered hundreds of corpses hanging from trees. Each wore a sign spelling out in German *"Ich bin ein Jude"* [I am a Jew]. The atrocities were committed on the orders of Joseph Stalin.

Whatever remained of any value, such as important papers, jewelry, family photo albums, many of the letters Helena had received from Hektor, her regular correspondence with Alphons von Bickel, the copy of *Gone with the Wind*, canned goods, pieces of clothing designated somewhat more acceptable than the everyday rags, were taken down to the vault. The curved stairway was then filled with broken crates, boxes, and other dry trash. It became a stairway to nowhere.

The distributor cap for the little Steyr was still nestled in Helena's purse. All they could do now was sit around and wait.

"What do you think will happen to us?" asked Hektor. Albert was just as interested in knowing what could occur. Their father spoke up before Helena had a chance to reply.

"I have an idea that the Allied soldiers will search every part of each house and make sure no one is hidden. They may physically search each of us. Conquering troops have to find out if there are weapons that could harm them. That's what our troops did. Once they discover that people are harmless, they may look around for spoils of war—not that there is much to reward them in this hovel!" Hektor was shifting from one foot to the other. He was terribly nervous about the whole experience. Helena immediately discerned his problem.

"Hektor, go to the bathroom this minute. I don't want to do unnecessary washing. Without doors, you won't miss anything. Just listen to what your father has to say! Tell him to use his choleric voice!"

"What do we do when we don't understand them? They will speak other languages. Most of them speak English, and others speak French," he yelled as he was running for the WC.

"True," said their father, raising his booming voice. "Not one of us speaks English, but your mother speaks a little French. With a bit of luck, she can be our interpreter. Perhaps one of the soldiers has German parents or grandparents in America and knows some German phrases. One never knows. We must make sure we make eye contact and try to read their facial expressions. You will be amazed how much information you can glean that way. Let's appear respectful but not browbeaten."

They heard the crunch of tanks as they mowed down any obstacles and maneuvered with considerable ease through the rubble that once was a street paved with cobblestones. The road was bare. Those who remained in town were huddled inside, waiting with uncertainty. Hektor and Albert went to their bedroom and peered from behind a blanket shielding two narrow windows facing the main drag. Alex had warned them.

"Whatever you do, do not move the blanket covering the windows. Just look through those small holes cut by the shrapnel. If those soldiers notice any movement, they might shoot at you."

The boys spotted the first of numerous tanks painted in a camouflage mixture of muddy brown and shades of olive green. Among this mélange of color, they noticed a black star and a red, white, and blue flag with a number of stars and stripes. They didn't know they were looking at an American flag.

All of a sudden they caught sight of several foot soldiers scurrying from house to house under the protection of the tanks. The top of the first tank popped open, and a very black man emerged. He was smiling from ear to ear and flashing his brilliant white teeth. Hektor and Albert were shocked. They never saw anyone that black before. Hektor and Albert were so excited they almost forgot their father's warning not to create any motion in the rug that shielded them from being seen by anyone on the outside.

"Boys, you come away from those windows this minute!" Helena hollered.

One of the soldiers used his machine gun to push aside the blanket at the front door. Not being met by any resistance and continuing the frantic pointing of his weapon to the left and right, he marched toward the next blanket, which led into the Birken apartment. Soon he conquered the castle of blankets and old rugs and faced Helena and Alex.

He seemed to be chewing on something. When he first spoke, they saw the lump in his left cheek. Then it moved to the right side of his face. Helena couldn't figure out what was happening. *Don't speak with your mouth full!* came to Helena's mind. However, that was not the approach she should resort to in the present situation.

The soldier sensed her curiosity. With that, he reached with his free hand up to his mouth, grabbing the lump of well-chewed gum and stretched it as far as the length of his arm allowed. The Birkens were amused. Only later did they discover what "that stuff" was called. The armed intruder realized no one understood what he was saying or asking. He frisked Alex first, then Helena, and finally the boys. Not detecting any guns, grenades, or knives, he began to relax a little. His eyes swept around the almost-barren room. He inspected the potbelly stove and smiled approvingly. When the Birkens later discussed the interaction with the soldier, they concluded he was trying to tell them that he had an oven like it in his own home in America.

He noticed that Alex was supporting himself on two canes. First he pointed at Alex, then at his canes, and then pretended he was firing his weapon out of one of the bedspread-veiled windows in the living room. What he was trying to learn was if Alex had been a soldier and was wounded during the war.

After a lot of shoving and grimacing, the affirmative nod conveyed to the intruder he guessed correctly. An approving smile flashed across his face. He touched his helmet with his right hand and saluted Alex. Obviously, it didn't matter that they had fought on opposing sides at one time. He motioned to Frau Birken to lead the way and followed her from room to room, carefully checking each crate or box. When they got to the store and he noticed the stairway full of trash, he started picking away at it. He turned toward Helena.

"All *Dreck?* All *kaput?*" She understood.

"*Ja, alles kaput.*" Luckily, he was gullible enough to believe her.

The whole thing lasted fifteen or perhaps twenty minutes at best. It seemed like an eternity to them. Satisfied he had encountered harmless civilians who seemed to be relieved by his neutral demeanor, the soldier moved up the stairway to pay a quick visit to the folks on the higher floors.

The neighbors were older people and looked scared out of their wits. The search in their apartments was even more perfunctory. As the Birkens learned later, the investigating soldier became somewhat annoyed with Julius Jokkish. Seeing Julius's radio, the soldier had pointed at it with his machine gun. The foolish man was trying to tell the soldier that it was "kaput."

He could tell the American didn't believe him. The soldier just walked over to the radio, picked it up sort of lovingly and set it on the floor. Then he gave it one swift kick smashing it to pieces. He looked up at Herr Jokkish and said, "Now kaput." He turned on his heels and left. Satisfied with his search of the first house on Kupfer-strasse, the soldier moved on to the next building.

He turned his attention on Herr Gutz's property, which was directly adjacent to the building that housed the Birkens' quarters. His building had a huge courtyard that separated the main house from a relatively large detached building. On the ground floor were Gutz's tea-processing business and a small textile factory operated by an older woman. The boys called her Aunt Theresa. At one time this building was the carriage house. Aunt Theresa lived in the quarters above her business; she was more or less a recluse but had always taken a shine to Hektor.

Hektor and Albert were watching through a slit in the blanket. Their eyes followed the soldier as he made his way toward the door leading to Aunt Theresa's business. Without glass dampening the sound, they could clearly hear shouting going on next door. They saw three POWs emerging from Aunt Theresa's factory. Like Helena, she was always kind to the captured men and helped them as much as she could without getting into trouble. The American approached the three Belgian POWs with caution. Somehow they managed to communicate to him that the old lady was OK, as was the woman in the store on the corner where he stopped first.

Herr Gutz was another story; he had taken advantage of their situation. They wanted to retaliate at this point. In their opinion, he was a mean German. Anyone who carefully watched the facial expressions and gestures of the POWs could tell what they were trying to convey to the American. They started wrecking everything belonging to Herr Gutz that had survived the bombings.

Huge bags of teas and herbs were dumped all over the courtyard as they laughed. Then they proceeded in a joint effort to beat the man himself. They hauled him out into the open and gave him a good licking in front of all who dared to watch. The American foot soldier didn't trust what his eyes beheld.

An American officer soon drove into the courtyard in a funny-looking vehicle. The boys saw their first Jeep. The officer jumped from the car and put an end to the fight. Next he was belting out all sorts of commands most watchers didn't understand. It became clear: Herr Gutz's courtyard was the designated spot for the canteen. Soon the aromas of cooking permeated the air.

Soldiers walked by the house, carrying their tinplates of food. Hektor and Albert were absolutely astonished.

"Have you ever seen bread that white? Or mustard that yellow? Or a wiener that big and long?" Hektor exclaimed.

"No!"

Most surprising was the bread; it looked light and fluffy and white as snow. Their mouths were salivating; it was so long since they had much more than their mother's brown soup. After they consumed the humble fixings their mother put before them, the boys headed for their room.

"Tonight you can take off your clothes and shoes. For the first time in months, you can sleep the whole night. We won't have to worry about running to the bomb shelter any longer. We may not have peace yet, but at least we will not have to scramble for our lives."

With those words on her lips, Helena said a prayer of thanks and pulled the cover over her boys. She finished the job with their much-needed featherbeds.

In June Grandpa Krämer sat down with his son-in-law.

"Franz, you have to find a way to get to that safe in the cellar at Ratsherrnweg. I never told you about my hidden treasure located under the large oriental rug. The only other person who knows of its existence is Mother. When they poured the cement floor in 1938, I told the builder to leave an oblong hole big enough for a later installation of a large generator. After we moved into the house, I sunk a safe into that space without outside help. As crippled as I was, it was one hell of a job. I was lucky Waltraute was still well and strong enough to give me a hand."

It was here Grandpa Krämer buried the remaining gold dating back to the days before he left to fight in 1915. Whatever coins were not needed to kick-start and float the Krämer enterprise during the 1920s were eventually moved to the well-hidden safe in their retirement villa.

When Franz Dimmelsburg unearthed the treasure in the summer of 1945, he had no idea that it held all of Grandma Krämer's jewels, valuable stock certificates and papers, and the remaining cigar boxes filled with twenty-mark gold coins issued in the late 1880s. Grandpa Krämer's stash had turned into the means by which they would survive.

Chapter 14

THE first months after the end of the war were rough on Helena. She had no trouble managing her own life during wartime. Now she had to deal with a handicapped husband. Alex was more of a burden than a help. The boys needed her attention too. The deprivations she and her family had to deal with nagged at her conscience—not that any of this was her fault. However, Helena often felt responsible for everyone's problems. The extended family looked for her help and counsel. She had difficulty coping with the abundance of negative issues placed on her shoulders. Often she would burst into tears and sob. Helena descended into the depths of depression. Her boys became frightened during such times. Before praying with her sons at night, their mother often gave voice to her personal feelings.

"If it wasn't for you boys, I would have left your father a long time ago or ended it all."

They recalled hearing her lamentations on several occasions since the closing days of the war. Hektor was too young to fully comprehend the implications. No one in the family recognized her cries for help. If psychiatry had been more advanced, they would have known that their mother was manic-depressive and perhaps even suffered from something that would later be termed PTSD. For now, the Birkens tried to make the best of the situation.

"When will I be able to go to school again?" Hektor asked every morning. Months went by without any schooling after the war ended.

"I don't know," Helena replied after she heard the question just once too often. "Since there isn't a safe site for you to play with your friends and so little is left around here for you to read, no one would be happier than your mother to send you off to school." *What a relief it would be not to have my bored boys underfoot. Having to keep useless Alex out of my hair is more than enough.*

At last they learned that school would resume in August 1945 at the Wackenburgschule. Helena was elated that Hektor could finally continue his education. Things had gotten too complicated. Albert chose to finish school in his grandparents' neighborhood. Eventually, he would start his apprenticeship with a master butcher in Rüttenscheid. With Albert gone, one of the twin beds stood vacant in the boys' bedroom.

An old friend, Lothar Zend, came calling. Lothar had lost his home in Düsseldorf during the last bombing. He was moving from door to door, looking for temporary housing.

"As you can see, I'm destitute and am living on the streets these days. I walked here all the way from Düsseldorf. My hope was that you and your home had survived. I need your help. Is there any way I could stay with you for a while until I can find a home of my own? I lost everything."

"Of course, Lothar. If you don't mind sharing a bedroom with Hektor, you are more than welcome to stay with us as long as you need to."

Her mind drifted off to her longtime friend Alphons von Bickel.

In her preoccupation with Alphons, she hadn't noticed the lecherous smile that had briefly crept across Lothar's face.

"Have you heard anything from Alphons since the end of the war?"

"Last I knew, he was living in the south. And no, I haven't seen him in a couple of years. He spent a few days with me in July 1943. We truly enjoyed being together."

"I'm surprised he didn't stop to see me when he was so close by in Düsseldorf. And he didn't mention his visit in any of his letters," mused Helena. Lothar just smiled and thought it was best not to discuss Alphons any further.

"Well, thank you for opening up your home to me. I won't mind at all sharing Hektor's bedroom. I like young boys; he won't be any trouble at all." There was that smile again.

Lothar was clearly older than Hektor's parents. He was somewhere in his early fifties, perhaps even older. Uncle Lothar was completely bald. His beady eyes looked through wire-rimmed glasses. He was middle-age paunchy. His body had seen better days.

Things went along fine for the first week. Hektor thought it was a bit strange that Lothar paraded around without a stitch of clothes before he hopped under his featherbed. He couldn't figure out the strange noises he would sense after the lights were turned off. A couple of times Hektor thought Lothar was moaning in his sleep and became concerned about his well-being. But he chose to cover his head with his giant down pillow to shut out the unwanted distractions that prevented him from falling asleep.

Eventually, Lothar became more comfortable with the sleeping arrangements and thought it was high time to teach Hektor all about the birds and the bees. After a few nights of being "instructed" by Uncle Lothar, Hektor knew something wasn't right. When he questioned what his uncle was doing, Lothar asked him not to share their bedtime adventures with the others in his family.

"Remember, we must keep some things just between us men.

There are things we just don't tell our mothers and fathers. What I'm teaching you is all about growing up."

Rarely did Hektor keep anything from his mother. Supposedly, the uncle was out looking for a job. Hektor took his mother aside right after lunch. He almost mouthed his words. Helena was tempted to tell him to speak up.

"Mutti, I need to speak with you. Maybe we can talk in our bedroom. That way no one else can hear what we are saying." Helena became concerned.

"What's this about? I'll be needed back in the store; I can't leave the apprentice alone for too long. I don't know where your father is. I hate asking him to do anything. Perhaps he's managed to get himself down to the cellar."

Hektor didn't want to postpone this particular talk with his mother. It had taken all of his courage to confront her with his problem.

"OK then, let's go. What's the big secret?"

"That's just it—a huge secret! Uncle Lothar is weird. Actually, I think he does some strange things. He doesn't put on a nightshirt or pajamas when he gets ready for bed. For a few nights now, he climbs into bed with me instead of getting into his own. He is stark naked. I've never even seen my own father without clothes, never mind a total stranger."

Helena was all ears. She thought she wasn't hearing correctly.

"Uncle Lothar started playing with his private part and wanted me to do the same. When I asked him what he was doing with his pee pee, he glared at me. 'My *Glockenspiel* isn't called a *pee pee*. It's called a *penis, prick, dick,* or *cock*. You are eleven years old, going on twelve. You should know better. Didn't your father ever teach you anything about how babies are made?' In his words, it was high time I learned. He would know how to teach me the right stuff I needed to stash away in my head.

"Then he told me, 'I've been playing with men and boys for years.

I want to teach you a few things. Who knows, you might like to join the club someday.' Last night he said that men didn't always want to make babies. That was the reason men often had fun with other men rather than with women; then he forced his stiff thing into my *Popo*. It hurt a lot, and I cried. When I showed him the blood on the sheets, he told me to say I had a bad nosebleed in my sleep. The things he says and wants me to do with him frighten me. From the moment he first touched me, he told me never to talk about anything he and I were doing in the bedroom—not to Albert or any of you. He said we needed to keep it our secret. If I spoke about it to anyone, I might be sorry. That really scared me."

For a split second, Hektor thought he was facing Ortrud in the second act of Wagner's *Lohengrin* as Helena screamed, *"Entweihte Götter!"* [Profaned Gods!].

"I can't believe what I'm hearing. Let me call your father! I can't fathom we invited a pervert and pedophile into our home. Just wait until your father hears what happened."

Hektor didn't know what his mother meant by the names she called Uncle Lothar. She yelled Alex's name loud enough to shake the rafters. When he finally found them standing in Hektor's bedroom, Helena told Alex the awful story.

"And to think, that good-for-nothing even threatened our son." For once Alex was the one who wanted to deal with the problem at hand.

"You tend to the store, Helena. I will handle Lothar." As soon as Lothar returned, Alex confronted him.

"Hektor shared with Helena in considerable detail the nighttime entertainment experienced with you. Don't tell me it's true."

"Yes, Alex, it's true. You must have been blind not to notice my fondness for boys and men. What I did with Hektor is no big deal. I thought it was high time for him to learn something about sex. I know how Helena feels about your sexual relationship with her. No wonder you were looking to get laid with that nurse in Baden-Baden.

She probably had to suck your cock, since you couldn't get on your knees or move your ass.

"Helena told our buddy Alphons and me not just once, 'I have been away from worldly things since Alex got me pregnant the last time in 1941.' She has even shared her opinions about sex with Albert. Helena views sex as an obligation, a nuisance, and goes so far as to say it is something dirty."

"I'm not here to discuss my sex life. I'm talking to you about what you did to Hektor. Don't change the subject."

"By the way, Alphons isn't a homosexual. His relationship with your wife was nothing but platonic. You didn't have to worry about him. Just read some of that drivel they wrote to each other through the years. I can guarantee there isn't a single 'fuck' in all that schmaltz.

"She told me all those lofty letters of theirs are saved in a big box down in that vault of yours. They are her most prized possessions, other than that damn book about the American South. All that intellectual talk about their mutual interests in literature, history, and politics was what kept her going through the years of strife and misery before and during the war. It was and is strictly a friendship between kindred minds."

"Lothar, that's your opinion. Right now, I'm not sure what to believe!"

"Alphons and I were drinking buddies during our younger years. Don't get me wrong. Had he shown the slightest interest, I would've been more than willing and able to ream his sorry ass. But as often as we shared hotel accommodations, nothing ever came of it—that is, he never responded to my overtures of wanting to screw him. He's now married, has fathered a few kids, and lives happily in the sunny South."

"Knowing what I know now, I'm beginning to have my doubts. I cannot completely accept what you are trying to make me believe."

"When I stopped at Helena's folks the other day to say hi to

Albert, he told me he positively detests Alphons von Bickel and holds him responsible for the frequent breakdowns in the relationship between you and Helena. He hates Alphons's guts. He is quite mature for going on fourteen; I wouldn't have tried to entertain him. As big as he is, he probably would have beaten the shit out of me had I laid a hand on him."

"Are you quite finished?" Alex was irate. He momentarily forgot his handicap. With a single burst of adrenaline, he swung his right crutch at Lothar. The first strike caused Lothar to lose his glasses. Before Alex lost his balance, he hauled off one more time. He got him where it hurts. Lothar moaned as he grabbed his crotch.

"Pack up your shit, and get your miserable prick out of my sight. Count your blessings I'm on these damn things; I'd kick you in your detestable balls and beat the hell out of you. Don't ever cross our threshold again."

Uncle Lothar was gone within fifteen minutes. Hektor was elated to see the last of Lothar.

Helena was glad school would start real soon. Hektor couldn't wait.

"You will have to get up early. Wackenburgschule is about five kilometers from our house. You have no other choice but walking. I'm glad Peter Siebenschneider lives across the street. He'll be going to the same school. He is in your grade, isn't he?"

"Yes, Mother. He's been my buddy since he came back from the Sauerland."

Helena continued. "Only one wing of the building is usable. They are accommodating just kids in first through eighth grades."

"I'll talk to Peter about it."

"Hey, Peter, what time do you think we need to start walking toward school? I'm glad they finally can teach us again. It's been far too long!"

"No later than seven fifteen; we don't want to be late on the first day. There are new streets to figure out, new schoolrooms to discover, and new teachers with whom we don't want to start off on the wrong foot. I'm glad you are that excited about school. Not me. I liked being free and able to just goof around!"

They unearthed their old and shabby leather backpacks. A few sheets of paper and some pencils were tucked in. None of these supplies had been used since Hektor and Albert left Köndringen in September 1944. Hektor's backpack, covered with some whitish slime, smelled awful.

"Mother, you can't be serious? Yuck—I won't take that ugly thing."

"Never mind the white stuff. It's just a little mildew. I'll wash it off with Persil and let it dry for a few hours. Your father can put brown shoe polish on it. He's good at that. It won't look so bad. You just wait and see. He'll do wonders with that old thing." Helena continued her gesticulating.

Walking to Wackenburgschule, Peter got Hektor's attention. "Where is Albert hiding these days? I see you are wearing that old pack after all. Actually, it doesn't look too bad. Your dad did a pretty good job of rejuvenating the darn thing."

"Albert spends much of his time with our grandparents at their partially restored old house in Rüttenscheid. He is finishing his last year of school in that neighborhood. It doesn't hurt my feelings he's gone so much. Lately, we did nothing but fight. At least I have some peace and quiet in our room.

They entered the building. All the kids were excited. One could tell by the racket they were making. The large classroom had forty dilapidated desks. Only a few seats in the front row were vacant.

"Let's grab these. I'd much rather sit in the last row," said Peter.

At eight o'clock, a man walked in. Peter elbowed Hektor. He whispered.

"Boy, he's a shrimp. I didn't think they made 'em that short. That crop of snow-white, wavy hair helps with his looks. Get a load of those large, scratched, horn-rimmed glasses. Too bad it's a guy! The women used to be much nicer. The men teachers often beat the shit out of me!" Their teacher got their attention by knocking on the desk closest to him.

"My name is Krantopf. I am your primary teacher for the foreseeable future." He had a firm but pleasant voice.

"Starting with you here in front of the class, I want your full names. Please spell them for me. I'm recording your names in alphabetical order. Starting tomorrow, I will assign your seats accordingly. You will keep your seats for one month; then we will rotate in the opposite direction."

The boys weren't too happy with that arrangement. After they thought about it, it wasn't such a bad idea. At least the same kids didn't get to always sit in the back and front rows of the class.

"Let's review your arithmetic. I'll start with the simple stuff. How much is nine times seven? Right—that is sixty-three. What if I said seventeen times eighteen? You don't need a pencil for that. Let me show you. Take the eight from eighteen and add it to the seventeen and hang on a zero. It becomes instantly two hundred fifty in your brain. Then all you do in a split second is multiply seven times eight and add the result, fifty-six, to the two hundred fifty. The correct answer is three hundred six. Let's try it. Here is thirteen times seventeen."

Peter raised his hand.

"So I add the seven from seventeen to thirteen, and that instantly becomes two hundred in my head after I hang on the zero. Then I add three times seven, which equals twenty-one, and the final answer must be two hundred twenty-one. Is that right?"

"Yes, the answer is two hundred twenty-one. You got it! You practice that, and you'll be real multiplication whizzes in no time flat. We need to do these exercises while your minds are sharp and fresh." The fifteen-minute break at ten o'clock didn't come soon enough.

"Boy, I haven't sat still on my ass for this long since Adolf gave his last obnoxious speech. I almost pissed in my pants," said Peter.

They were standing down a way from Krantopf, who was taking a leak in the men's room.

"Let's catch some fresh air, Hektor. Aren't those guys standing over there sitting in the back row? Look at them—pissing against the wall and having a smoke. Have you tried smoking?"

"No, but Albert has. He got caught by Grandpa Krämer. First he got a whipping with that damn willow cane. He made him smoke that stogy of his, and me too. Both of us threw up. That miserable old man was happy teaching us that lesson."

"Those guys are lucky Krantopf pissed in the men's room. He probably couldn't hold it any longer. I'm surprised they don't have a teacher watching the playground. If they had, those kids would be in deep shit. We better get back to our seats. I'm sorry we won't be sitting together after today."

"I wonder what he has planned for us next," Hektor said. Krantopf marched back into class.

"Who in class has heard of Goethe and Schiller? What about Shakespeare? How many of you have started to learn English?"

Hektor waved his hand. "Yes, young man, what's your name again?"

"I am Hektor Birken."

"What are you trying to tell me?"

"A neighbor of ours, Herr Dorn, was a prisoner of war in England. He learned to speak the language. I befriended him and have picked up some phrases. My mother wants me to take private classes with him real soon."

"Good for your mother. We won't have time to teach you English at this school for years. Our subjects will be the basics of reading, writing, and arithmetic. We need to catch up; so much valuable time was lost during the last years!" At three o'clock, Hektor and Peter were ready to head home.

"I tell you, my dad talks about lumps on his ass called hemorrhoids. Sitting on those hard benches for all these hours, I might give him competition."

Herr Krantopf passed out booklets to take home to read. They each got one and left in a hurry. Hektor's booklet was an introduction to the famous German writer Johann Wolfgang von Goethe.

Looking at his teacher's handout, Helena approved of the home assignment.

"It's too bad—my entire collection of Goethe's opus is still crated up in Köndringen." In due time, Hektor received a good grade for his hard work. Hektor's paper was lauded by Krantopf in front of the whole class, but he didn't appreciate being singled out by his teacher.

Chapter 15

IN early October 1945, Helena Birken's thoughts turned southward toward her precious belongings. Anything of value was stored for more than two years at the Gasthaus Lion in Köndringen. Her predictions indeed had come true. There was no mail, telephone service, transportation for civilians, or long-distance communication.

Helena had tried to learn something about the condition of their friend Klara. Her efforts were in vain. The Helena of wartime gutsiness sprung into action. The matter at hand pulled her out of her deep depression. She had a cause to fight for. One early morning, she announced at the breakfast table.

"I can no longer wait to learn what happened. I am going down to Köndringen and find out for myself." Helena decided on her move as soon as she learned that Albert planned to spend a few days at home.

"Albert, the first day of your potato vacation, you and I are hopping on a coal train from the freight depot in Essen West." The whole family, including Albert, who was thirteen going on thirty, was speechless.

"Just look at you. You aren't a kid any longer. You have turned into a young man in the last year. I need your help. Hektor is too young and small, and your dad can't do anything."

No one offered any objections. Helena had made up her mind. Her legwork was complete. Helena consulted with one of her regular customers working for the railway in North-Rhine Westphalia. His work involved restoration and repair of train tracks, platforms, and facilities at the hub in Essen West. Helena ignored the others and dealt strictly with Albert.

"My customer gave me an idea as to which coal trains are passing through, which are stopping to add more cars filled with precious hard coal to be sent to France, and which are headed in the right direction for our purposes."

On the morning of October 6, Mother Birken and Albert left on their adventure long before daylight and well hidden by darkness. Helena was on a mission. Each carried a bag containing a couple of changes of underwear, an extra shirt and sweater, a wash cloth and a piece of awful-smelling soap, a toothbrush and toothpaste, and a roll of sandpaper-like toilet paper.

"Sorry, son, all I have is that lousy *Kommissbrot* [army bread], a hunk of cheese, some hard salami, and a thermos with hot chicory coffee. I'm looking forward to better things once we get to Aunt Klara's place."

In addition, they rolled up a piece of oilcloth and stuck it in one of the bags; they might use it to sit on or as additional cover in case of rain. They both carted an old and well-worn collapsible pre-World War II umbrella. Here and there, they turned on their flashlights as they walked quietly along the dark streets taking them to the railway station.

"It's a good thing we brought the flashlights," said Albert.

"Yes, otherwise we might break an ankle or worse before we even get started." Most sidewalks were still in bad shape, and many streets were not much better.

Arriving at Essen West, they carefully skirted the station itself. They walked across the tracks leading north and walked on the southern track for several meters. Helena's informer told her where and beside which marker she and Albert should stand to await the arrival of the coal train headed south.

"Are you sure Herr Hasenpfeffer gave you the right information?" asked Albert.

"Oh yes, he is a reliable person. I have known him for years. He's been a regular customer of ours since we started the business."

Sure enough, at four thirty they heard the noisy steam locomotive from a considerable distance. With lots of huffing and puffing, the monstrous creature pulled by them and gradually slowed to a halt. They stood about fifteen cars down from the engine. Helena and Albert couldn't see anyone.

"What's all that commotion at the end of the train?" Helena whispered.

"Mother, they're adding a bunch of coal-filled cars. I can barely understand what you're saying with all that noise." Helena seized the opportunity.

"This car has those grab bars the guy talked about. Let's use them like a ladder and hop on the wagon. Get moving. Make sure the freight car is filled with coal before you hop down. The coal will be forgiving on your butt. Let's do it like we rehearsed on our walk to the station." Albert went up the bars first.

"Hold on to my hand. I'll pull you behind me. Let me quickly flash this light to make sure the wagon has coal." He held the flashlight just below the rim inside the railway car.

"Yes, there's coal for sure. It's not very deep. You'll be OK, Mom. I'll jump first. I'll try catching you." After their safe landing, they just sat for a moment. Helena let all the air escape from her lungs.

"I'm proud of our achievements so far. It's a good start, son. I don't know how this whole adventure will play out. I doubt we'll be back in time for the resumption of school." Albert responded.

"Let's just sit here quietly in the depressions we made in the loose coal. Once we are moving, we'll find better seats." He couldn't help snickering, feeling the sharp edges of the crushed coal pressing on his butt through his relatively thin pants.

"Daylight will make our scouting efforts easier. We want to make sure we sit deep enough not to be spotted by anyone observing us from a distance. I wish we packed a couple of small cushions. My ass is beginning to smart."

They sat there for what seemed like an eternity. Finally, they survived the last of the noisy, jerky movements as the cars were coupled. With dawn and the first glimmer of daylight, they noticed the coal was heaped in the center. There were relatively deep areas in all the corners.

"Let's sit in the northeast corner of the wagon with our backs against the wall. We'll be protected against the elements and the jerkiness," volunteered Helena.

Between Cologne and Bonn, the train came to an abrupt halt. They listened to the shouting voices of train personnel but didn't dare look. They huddled quietly in their corner. So far they were lucky. No one had spotted them. The weather gods were kind. There were some gray clouds but no signs of rain. They resolved this was a good time to take some nourishment—not exactly a champagne brunch, but the bread with some cheese and salami tasted awfully good. They both had a few sips of the hot beverage; calling it coffee was an exaggeration. Nevertheless, it was something warm in their bellies.

They listened quietly to each other's eating noises. The railway crew discussed the reason for the stoppage.

"Must be some important big shot among the British or American armed forces laying claim to the track," said a guy just outside their coal car.

"Yeah, they pretty much run the show these days," echoed another unseen voice.

After an hour or so, the train slowly resumed its motion on the single track headed south. While their freight train was sidetracked, occupation troops were given the right-of-way. It happened again south of Mannheim. There were more of the off-handed comments. At least they were in the know about why the train stopped.

The second night on the train was not as charitable. Early in the evening, a steady rain started to pelt them as they sat on coals. Some of the coal dust mixed with the blowing rain settled on their faces; they looked like escapees from a mine. They were thankful for their umbrellas and the oilcloth they had tented over themselves. Helena laughed at her son.

"Albert, you look like Peter, our chimney sweep."

They approached Karlsruhe in the early morning hours. The rain gave way to thick fog. As they came to a sudden stop in the former freight yard, they jumped from the coal car, home sweet home for the last forty-eight hours. Helena had guts enough to approach one of the railway people.

"Kind man, I need your help. My son and I have been stowaways on that coal train from Essen for the last couple of days. Can you steer us in the right direction to catch the best train that will get us to Köndringen? We are hoping to retrieve our things that were stored in the little village. We have no idea what happened there toward the end of the war."

"Ma'am, you realize you are now in the French zone. The provisional French government of this zone is seated in Baden-Baden, a little south of here. You said you came from Essen? Well, in Karlsruhe and north of here the bombing was much worse than the stretch from Baden-Baden to Freiburg. True, there were some bombings of these cities but nothing like you experienced. Also, there are two railway tracks between Freiburg and Baden-Baden with somewhat limited freight traffic.

"I suggest you catch the train on the southern track over there; one should be coming through here in about an hour. It won't stop in Köndringen. There is no industrial interest there. Freight trains only stop for scheduled pickups. The one you are catching will halt in Emmendingen, about five kilometers further south. Now Ma'am, I have to get going. I'll be busy with detaching and attaching some freight cars and will look the other way. Good luck with the retrieval of your things."

With a hearty *Grüß Gott* [greet God], he turned on his official heels as Helena and Albert walked in the direction they were told to take.

At nine thirty the freight train headed toward Emmendingen rolled into the yard. They had their eye on the middle and hopped on as soon as it stopped moving. It was a sort of cattle car—at least it smelled of animal when they slid back the door and entered.

As their eyes wandered around the freight car, they noticed some straw and what appeared to be animal droppings. On closer inspection, they realized that they were human feces. Even more to their surprise, they met a fellow traveler.

Actually, it was a young woman with a baby. They were all astounded as they faced each other. The young woman was sparsely clad in a filthy housedress made from the cheapest floral cotton. The infant, held closely to the mother's bosom, was just as dirty. They became aware of the baby's suckling sounds. Albert looked away. Helena became engaged immediately.

"Why are you traveling with a baby on a freight car?"

"I could ask you the same question except you are traveling with a young man. I was living with my husband in Wiesbaden when he was drafted right after his eighteenth birthday last October. He was never heard from again. I gave birth to our son four months ago. I'm returning to my parents' farm outside of Emmendingen. There was no other way to travel but to take my chances on a freight car."

"You have a better reason to be on this train than my son and I. We're on our way to retrieve things. I hope you and your child will be reunited with your loved ones soon."

Thank goodness there were no more stops along the way between Karlsruhe and Emmendingen. The train pulled into the freight yard. All of them emerged from the smelly conveyance as quickly as possible. They said a quick goodbye, wishing each other success in the days to come. Albert knew the way from the station to the main road. Good thing they were only carrying their carpetbags. Closer to their destination, they noticed the storks' nest was empty.

"They must have left for Africa already," said Albert.

He was disappointed not to experience once again the annual spectacle. At least the church steeple was still there to greet them, as was the whole familiar village. Nothing had happened there in terms of bombing. Everything he knew had its familiar look. He gratefully exclaimed, "The Lion stands proudly!"

The Shell gas station was not operational, but the inn was open. Helena and Albert ascended the well-worn sandstone steps on the south side of the entrance and walked into the inn. They were a sight to behold. Their clothes were filthy and raggedy, and their faces bore smudges of coal and dust. As they appeared in the doorway, Klara was behind the bar, drawing a beer for a patron. The glass almost slipped out of her hand as she spotted Albert and then Helena.

"Oh my God, you are alive! I can't believe what I am seeing!"

With that, she set the half-drawn beer down and swept from behind the bar. She drew Albert to her and hugged him, much to his thirteen-year-old dismay. Klara didn't care; she was so elated to see one of her boys alive. And then the two women embraced in a knowing manner. They understood each other without saying a word. Their body language spoke of the outward manifestation of celebrating the fact they all lived.

"How did you get here? How are Hektor and Alex? I presume they are in Essen, and they are OK?" Helena wasn't sure which questions to answer first. She took her good time.

"All of us survived the war except three of my cousins. We still have not heard anything about my brother. Have you gotten any word about Rudi?" Helena hesitantly asked. Klara tried to hold back her tears.

"He was never heard from after he left for the eastern front in September 1944. I'm almost sure I'll never see him again."

As Klara was busy fixing breakfast, Helena related the events of their travels by freight train. Klara was amazed by Helena's bravado. She dished up the warm breakfast of scrambled eggs with ham and some of her hearty bread. What a treat! Mother Birken said a prayer of thanks for all the blessings they had experienced. When they finished the meal, Helena couldn't wait.

"What happened in here as the war drew to its inevitable end?"

"Helena, everything is upstairs—that is, almost everything. Your belongings are not necessarily in the same condition in which you left them. Still, most things are waiting for you."

"Don't keep me on pins and needles, Klara. What happened when the troops marched through the village last spring?"

"Let's have a glass of wine. It will make it easier to relive the day." Klara poured healthy glasses of house wine for Helena and herself.

"Albert, would you like some apple juice?"

"Thank you, that would be great." All set with their drinks, Klara continued.

"As the last week of the war drew near, I knew I was not going to leave my humble home. I was going to face the conquering troops— well, almost face them. I looked for a suitable hideout—close but not too close to the house. I settled on the cellar under the barn at the end of the courtyard. It has an unobtrusive clap-door entry. I camouflaged it with pig manure. I hid some food items and liquid refreshments in the cistern. If worse came to worse, I could always open a bottle of wine. Rudi stored all his prized vintages in that cave. Leaving the clap-door open just a crack, I could observe the courtyard and a good portion of the house and inn."

"My God, Klara, weren't you scared being that close to the house?"

"Late in the morning, a truck pulled into the courtyard. Ten soldiers jumped from the vehicle. They stormed the house. Six of them were white. The other four were very dark, perhaps Moroccan. All of them spoke French. They all carried guns with bayonets fixed. I heard them enter the pub, yelling at the discovery of the liquid refreshments. All I could hear was this constant jubilant noise. *Vive la France, Vive la France* [long live France] was their favorite slogan."

"Did you say ten soldiers invaded the inn? Just think—they might have raped you."

"I had no idea what was going on. They moved down to the cistern underneath the pub. They must have discovered the kegs of beer and the huge barrels of wine. They sang at the top of their voices. I figured they drank themselves into a stupor.

"A couple of hours went by. Suddenly I saw naked men charging up and down the hallway on the second floor. The windows were partially open. Now I really heard what went on. I do speak and understand a little French. I eavesdropped on their hooting and hollering. First, they went into my bedroom and the one where you boys slept. Every drawer was emptied on the floor. All my linens and clothes were strewn up and down the hall. The money and jewelry they were seeking were with me in the secret wine cellar. Next they headed down the hall to the room where your things were stored. One of the dark guys kicked in the door with his bare feet.

"They bayoneted all doors on the wardrobe, which was essentially empty except for Alex's uniforms and suits. They took those as wartime souvenirs. They tried the same approach on your beautiful buffet. When the doors wouldn't give, they took off the back. Finding the thing completely empty, they were cussing. Two of the guys picked up your sewing machine and tossed it into the beds. It had a soft landing in the down featherbeds; no harm was actually done. A third soldier took his bayonet and scraped something all over the top of your buffet. The one and only crate they broke open was that with your precious linens. Those joined mine along the hallway.

"I hate to tell you, but they pissed, shit, and threw up all over everything. Close up, it was quite a sight when I finally was able to see the mess they left. Their shenanigans went on for several hours before they determined they'd done their share of conquering. One of the guys yelled, *'J'emmerde cet endroit, mec, je me casse'* [I'm getting the fuck out of here]. The driver backing the truck into the road barely missed one of the old posts of the ancient gate.

"When things quieted down at last, I dared to come out of hiding. I couldn't believe my eyes when I went down to the cellar under the pub. These guys apparently opened the gaskets on several wine barrels and flooded the room. There were still pieces of their underwear floating in the mixture of red and white wine and beer. I don't have any doubt they took a swim in the alcoholic bathtub they had created. I'm convinced their drunkenness precluded them from grasping the true value of things when they entered the room with your belongings. Well, let me take you upstairs."

They climbed the old wooden stairway to the second floor. Klara took out her key and unlocked the door. There stood the twin master bedroom set with its plump featherbeds and pillows, looking just the way she left it. She saw the damage done to the huge wardrobe fashioned from black Caucasian walnut. She read the inscription left on the top of her buffet, *Vive la France*—a permanent reminder of the conquering troops.

"That was so stupid of me to lock all these empty pieces of furniture. Well, the damage is done. It could be worse."

As her eyes swept the room, she noticed her Pfaff and the crates with books, linens, silver, and china. They all seemed to be intact. She turned to face Klara with an expression of pure joy because most of her family treasures had survived the war.

"How can we ever thank you for all you did for the boys and for us? You and Rudi were a godsend!"

They went downstairs and sat at the large round table in the corner of the inn. Helena and Albert sat there simply spellbound by Klara's reliving the end of the war. She continued.

"I know not everything is perfect. As a matter of fact, I just washed and boiled all of your linens after they cleared out. They are not pressed or mangled, but they are clean. You will have to finish the job when you have access to a mangle some day."

There would be so many things Helena needed to do some other day. For now, she had to concentrate on finding a way to get her things back to Essen.

"Klara, do you know if the company that handled our move down here still exists in Emmendingen?"

"I believe so, since the town was hardly touched by the war. Why don't you and Albert hop on my bike in the morning and find out what they can do for you?"

The five-kilometer stretch seemed much shorter on the bike. Albert recalled walking the same road for the first time when he and Hektor went to the circus on a dark and spooky night. After a couple of inquiries about the location of the moving company, they found their way. Helena immediately recognized Herr Spandau.

"Oh yes, we are still in the moving business, although most of it is rather local these days due to all the restrictions imposed on us by the French government and the condition of roads and railroad tracks."

"Can you give me any encouragement regarding the transport of my belongings from Köndringen to Essen?"

"The first thing you need to do is obtain a permit from the provisional French government in Baden-Baden allowing you to move your things out of the French zone, through the American zone, and into the British zone. They will also have to approve the use of a flatbed freight car for the purpose of hauling a moving van—not a small order. You have your work cut out for you. Come and see me if you are successful at securing the needed documents. Good luck, Frau Birken!"

Helena and Albert looked down in the dumps when they returned to the Lion. They related what they had learned from Herr Spandau. Klara realized she had to take charge.

"Helena, I think you should try hitching a ride with someone who is headed in the direction of Baden-Baden first thing tomorrow. I suggest you go alone and leave Albert with me. We can pack up whatever needs crating or boxing. There is a milk truck that runs early in the morning. I know the driver; he probably won't mind someone to talk to on his daily run. He drops off his load in Offenburg and certainly will know a way of getting you to Baden-Baden."

"Can you think of anything that might open a few doors for me? You know how worthless our money is and needing something with me in terms of greasing a few palms."

"Don't worry, I had planned to give you a couple of bottles of Kirschwasser and a box of Rudi's best cigars. The booty ought to make a few things possible."

And thus began the next leg of Helena's long journey. Ernst, the driver of the milk truck, was kind of quiet. When she asked him if he smoked, he replied with a nod. She gave him a few of the precious cigars.

"I won't smoke in the cab of the truck. I'll just sniff the unlit cigar. When I want a better taste, I'll suck on this wonderful treat."

Helena could tell he was in tobacco heaven. He was perfectly happy and savored the moment when he could light up as soon as he pawned Helena off on another driver in Offenburg.

Helena Birken arrived at the appropriate office in Baden-Baden at ten thirty in the morning. She gained entry to the person in charge by bribing his secretary with a few cigars. Her husband would be thrilled with them, the woman assured Helena as she beckoned her to follow her to the superior's office.

Herr Hackensack sat behind a large desk, shuffling papers from one side of the desk to the other.

"Come in, come in. What can I do for you? Have a seat. Although you are a bit on the short side, I still don't like looking up at people. After a while, it hurts my neck. Now, ma'am, what did you start to say?"

"My name is Helena Birken. My personal things and furniture were stored during the war at a friend's home in Köndringen. I am anxious to have them moved back to Essen. I understand that I need to obtain authorization and a bill of lading from your offices. Is that correct? I truly would appreciate your help in this matter."

"Well, my dear lady, that is quite a request you have there. I'm not sure if I can just issue these documents without first seeking approval by my French superiors. You realize they like to know and keep control over what is being moved out of their zone of jurisdiction."

He kept staring at Helena's large bag, making some sniffing sounds. "I see, you have a sizable satchel with you. Do I dare ask what you might be carrying with you?"

What a brazen scuzzball, Helena thought.

"Actually, I thought you might enjoy a bottle of this wonderful Kirschwasser; and as a man in your position, some good cigars wouldn't hurt your feelings either."

"Now you're talking, Frau Birken. Let me call my secretary. I believe we will be able to help you promptly."

Helena almost kissed him, but she was turned off by his snotty mustache. He dictated a memo giving Mrs. Birken permission to move her personal belongings from Köndringen to Essen. The document was typed on official stationery, and a large seal of the provisional French government was embossed onto the paper. Further, she was issued a bill of lading authorizing the use of a flatbed freight car for the purpose of executing the move.

"Thank you, Herr Hackensack. Thank you."

Helena, rarely given to expressions of an emotional nature with total strangers, could have hugged both of them. Instead, she grabbed their hands and thanked them repeatedly and profusely. She floated out of the office building with the treasured papers in her possession.

Her euphoria evaporated quickly when she contemplated her return trip to Köndringen. Perhaps she might be fortunate enough to catch a ride back.

As luck had it, the trucker who had given her a lift from Offenburg was about to make his return run. This time, she noted he had a young woman sitting in the cab up front. In addition, there were several other women and men of varying ages making the journey. With the exception of the young woman up front, they found themselves sitting on the floor in the back of the truck. "Mother Courage" thought the driver deserved a few cigars for his willingness to take her on.

Thirty minutes later, as they were driving along a heavily wooded area, the vehicle came to a sudden stop. The road was barricaded by a large wooden beam, and several soldiers emerged from the woods. They yelled, *descendre du camion* [get off the truck], and *où est notre identification* [where is your ID]? The commands were directed at all, including the driver. Gesturing and pointing at some sample papers, they got the idea across that everyone needed to show ID as to residing in or traveling with permission through the French zone.

Needless to say, Helena had no such papers. She was standing close to the end of the line of the victims being inspected. She took the formal letter she was issued that morning and folded it in such a way that the official seal appeared prominently. When it came her turn to be interrogated, she flashed her official French seal and resorted to a couple of French phrases.

As she was being spoken to, Helena couldn't help noticing that both guys standing in front of her had their flies wide open. It was evident that they weren't wearing anything under their uniforms.

Helena almost shrieked when one of the guys grabbed his erect penis, flashing it at his captive audience. They appeared to be ready for action.

Helena wanted to tell them "XYZ" or zip up. She was too scared and looked away. She was glad she was not as young as the other women. Helena could not believe her good fortune when she was waved back onto the truck. Everyone was allowed to continue the journey except three young women, including the one who had been seated next to the driver. Without saying a word, they all knew what was in store for those held behind.

Shaken by the events of the day, Helena wasn't so sure if she could face any more adventures on the last leg of her return trip. She stood for a long time by the country road, shivering in a steady rain before a driver came along who was kind enough to pick her up.

"I'm driving to Emmendingen. I know the Lion Inn; I'll drop you off right in front."

"Thank God." She said a few silent, heartfelt prayers as the truck began to move. Before she alighted from his chariot, she rewarded him with the second bottle of Kirschwasser and the remaining cigars.

"Well, that's a nice surprise. Glad I was able to help you, ma'am." Klara's bribes had done their trick.

Triumphantly, she entered the Lion waving the all-important papers for everyone to see. When she shared her exploits of the day with Klara and the patrons, they applauded her for her successful completion of the task.

The next morning she was off to Emmendingen on Klara's bike. Herr Spandau was shocked to see her so soon. Furthermore, he was astounded at her success.

"What did you do? How did you manage to get those papers? I just can't believe you did it!"

"Well, I did. How soon can you move on getting the flatbed car and a van to transport our things?"

"I will need at least a couple of days. I can have a moving van in Köndringen day after tomorrow. Getting the flatbed car and scheduling a hookup will take some doing. I will try my best to get you out of here as fast as possible."

Helena was elated! Good fortune was still on her side. The bike almost flew along the five kilometers back to the Gasthaus Lion. Klara was delighted Helena was successful in arranging for the return trip of her belongings. The happenings of the last few days deserved a celebration.

"Helena, I cannot think of a better way to enjoy this day. Let me open one of Rudi's favorite vintages." Klara poured the golden libation. They enjoyed reminiscing about the events that brought them together; they laughed and cried because not all was joyous or ended happily.

Three days later, Herr Spandau was there to load the moving van. When all was safely stashed on the vehicle, they transported it to the railway station, seated it on the flatbed, and sealed it securely overnight. The next morning Helena and Albert would enter the van and travel with their belongings. Taking heed of Herr Spandau's suggestion, they wouldn't leave the van unattended on the long journey to Essen.

Helena and Albert returned to the Lion; Klara was sweeping the steps from the second floor to the main entry. She seemed depressed.

"Is anything wrong, Klara?" Helena inquired.

"Yes and no! You won't believe this. A few minutes after you and Herr Spandau left with the moving van, a couple of French officers inspected the inn and all my facilities. It met with their approval. They informed me the building was seized for official purposes for an undetermined amount of time. Officers and their wives will occupy the three largest rooms. Actually, two of them will move in with their wives. The two who spoke with me came right out and told me they were lovers and lived together.

"I was taken aback, but the French don't see these matters quite so tragically. *C'est la vie*. I will be obliged to house, feed, and care for all of them. They are providing the food, but I will have to prepare meals for and clean up after them. Can you imagine what would have happened to your belongings if they saw them? Every last thing would have been shipped off to France—I can guarantee that! Helena, you have a sixth sense. I just cannot fathom your good fortune."

Neither could Helena. She was relieved and sad at the same time. What a terrible karma had befallen her helpful friend. Yes, Klara was upset at first. She also came to see a positive side to the invasion of her privacy. It gave her reason to go on with her life; it also gave her companionship that she had never dreamed of. While the French conquerors could be obnoxious, they were people doing their duty. She was sure they would have much preferred to be home in France. Klara accepted her situation and made the best of it.

After another sad farewell the next morning, Helena and Albert started their trek back to Essen. They were safely ensconced in the van sitting upon the flatbed freight car. They fixed the sliding door with a heavy chain, leaving it only slightly ajar for some fresh air. A couple of bales of straw became their beds, and Klara gave them ample provisions for the journey home.

Whenever the train halted along the way, they could almost count on someone trying to pry open the sliding door of the van. The intruders were surprised to discover that it was guarded by a chain. What shocked them was Helena Birken's appearance at the opening.

"What do you want? You have no business trespassing. I am accompanying my personal property legally. If you don't beat it promptly, I will yell for the conductor; he and the train personnel will take care of you. My son and I have train tickets and have a right to be on this conveyance. You have no business anywhere on this train."

She might have been little but never took any guff from others. She had not brought her belongings through the war and postwar hazards to be defeated by thieves and carpetbaggers. Once they met the wrath of Helena Birken, they crawled away, waiting for the next train and easier pickings. Helena realized quickly that Herr Spandau knew what he was talking about.

She was also thankful to Klara for her suggestion to take one of her larger chamber pots on board the train. It made for a more civilized manner of relieving themselves than it had been on their journey south. Whenever she had successfully dealt with unwanted intruders during train stoppages, she would take the opportunity to empty the pot. After her first attempt at being a trained sanitary agent in broad daylight, running into one of the men working the train, she opted to defer future disposals to nighttime. One time she was tempted to bless a particularly nasty invader of the coach with the contents of the chamber pot but thought the better and just scared him away with a barrage of words.

On the fourth day, they were finally unhitched from the freight train in Essen West late in the afternoon. After the motion of the train stopped, they experienced the lengthy maneuver of uncoupling their car from the train. Eventually, Helena and her treasures were safely parked on a dead rail.

"Albert, I want you to walk home by yourself. Let your father know where I am. I will stay until the van is picked up. Don't worry; I'll be OK. There still is plenty to eat and drink. More importantly, it's a good thing you thought of emptying our pot before the train came to a halt. Smile! I'm just fine!"

She was not going to leave the van sitting alone. Helena had not come this far to lose everything on her home turf.

Albert was greeted happily. His father could not grasp some of the stories he told. When Hektor asked if he could spend the last night with his mother in the railroad car, his father wasn't so sure. Finally, he gave in and let him take the walk to the railway station. Albert described exactly where the wagon was sitting on the dead rail. Hektor bundled up in his old navy pea jacket, picked up a flashlight, and was on his way in short order.

He had no difficulty finding the freight car. His mother didn't trust her ears when she heard the knock at the sliding door.

"Not again," she voiced.

When she peered out the narrow slit and discovered it was Hektor, Helena was delighted. She was glad she didn't have to spend this last night on the train alone.

"How nice you can partake of at least a small portion of the adventure of a lifetime." She had reached the end of a very long journey indeed.

After the local moving company successfully delivered her priceless possessions to the house on Kupferstraße, she could say in all earnestness, "All's well that ends well."

Chapter 16

HELENA Birken's opinion about the importance of confirmation in a Protestant's life was well known by family members. One might get married several times but was confirmed only once. Nothing deterred her from making her sons' confirmations major family events. It took some doing, but she succeeded on both occasions. The dry run for Hektor's celebration was Albert's coming of age in 1946.

"Mother, this whole thing is a royal pain. It's important to you, but not to me. I can't stand that Tranig character. Having to listen to that ass for a whole year is truly a challenge. You have no idea what it takes for me to sit there and listen to him pontificate. If I had to walk, I would never attend those damn classes of his. I'm counting my blessings. If Uncle Franz had not found that old bicycle for me, I would not be in Tranig's confirmation class."

"Young man, you are speaking to your mother. I expect you to be more respectful. Would you want me to discuss this with your grandfather?"

"He knows how I feel. He told me he wouldn't walk to those classes either. It's important to Grandma and you. Not to the males in this family."

Albert knew better than to oppose his mother or his grandmother. They were both cut from the same cloth. The weekly tutorials started in the fall of 1945. Albert reluctantly partook of the endlessly long sessions. There were forty-five to fifty other kids his age in the group. Pastor Tranig, in his wishy-washy manner, had his hands full.

Weeks before the confirmation, numerous commitments needed to be made. *How was the boy to get a decent dark suit for the event?* Helena discussed the matter with her father.

"I'll take care of that. My first grandson will have a proper suit on the occasion of wearing his first manly long pants. Among the stuff Mother sent to Swabia were several quality pieces of cloth. You know her—she always managed to have things in reserve. You're still in touch with the tailor, Wibbelschnitz, aren't you?"

"Yes, he managed to stay in our neighborhood. This blue-black striped material will make a fine confirmation suit. If it's OK with you, I will take it tonight. Wibbelschnitz will be able to measure Albert and get started. He doesn't have much to do these days. Few people have material for new things. I suppose he does many alterations." She didn't mention a word of the discussions she had earlier with her son.

Studying the catechism and the Bible were utterly boring for most children. Nevertheless, every good Protestant was subjected to the treatment. They had to pass muster in front of a large segment of the congregation. The test was always scheduled on a Sunday afternoon two weeks before Easter. Members of the confirmation class were expected to know certain Bible passages and all parts of the catechism by heart.

Pastor Tranig was in his glory when he could pick names and tasks at random.

"Just watch what that imbecile does when one of us can't recite all those useless verses."

"Albert, stop using that language when you are speaking about our pastor!"

"Sorry, Mother. He seems to enjoy catching those of us who have not adequately studied that stuff he finds so important. I'm not worried about the grilling like some of the kids in class. It ain't traumatic for me to miss a few passages. I'm ready to tell him, I'm an atheist. It doesn't faze me at all to miss or misspeak certain quotations from the Bible. Who the hell cares?"

"I care. Sometimes you are an embarrassment to the family. Hektor has made up his mind. Pastor Tranig will not get the better of him when his turn comes in two years."

"Well, that's his business. I'm glad I survived this little episode. All else ought to be a cinch."

"I wish you studied just a bit more; I was sitting on pins and needles for the entire three hours. Every time Pastor called your name, I could have sunk into the floor when you were floundering and getting lost in the readings. At this juncture, I share your view. I'm glad the test is over," said Helena.

The following weekend brought the big day. On the Thursday before confirmation Sunday, Albert and Robert Siepmann, a young butcher in the neighborhood, took a bike ride into the country. The Siepmanns had relatives in the Münsterland who were farmers. Robert knew they would be able to barter for a calf. Grandpa Krämer sprung a few of his gold coins; they always did the trick on the black market. Robert did the bartering with his uncle.

"My friend's grandfather is willing to pay you in gold. How much do you want for that black-and-white calf standing by the feeding trough?"

"How big are the coins?"

"They are twenty-mark pieces dating back to 1888."

"Two of them will do it. Let me see them!"

Robert turned to Albert. "He's letting us have that beauty for two of the coins. Is that OK with you?"

"Sure is. Here are the coins. Pay your uncle, and let's get the job done."

The uncle examined the coins carefully with glee in his eyes. Albert and his buddy killed the "golden calf" that became the main attraction of the confirmation feast. They butchered the animal at the farm and cut it up into manageable pieces. Half a calf was hauled on the backs of each of their bicycles for about sixty-five kilometers.

"You think you can handle the weight on the bike?" Robert wanted to know.

"I sure can. It's no heavier than hauling my brother around. At least that dead calf won't give me any guff!"

They left the farm late in the afternoon and entered the city after dark. No one stopped them or asked any questions regarding their treasured cargo.

Hektor and Klarissa had a different mission. Klarissa had been household help for years. Her sister worked at the British Officers' canteen on Wolfsbachweg. She approached one of the men with whom she became closely acquainted.

"My sister works with very nice people. Their older son is being confirmed this Sunday. Do you think it might be possible for me to buy a few cases of beer from the canteen with your help? These folks would surely appreciate it."

The Brit's face reflected a broad smile. "My mother made a big event of my confirmation a goodly number of years ago. I understand. Tell your sister to be here after dark on the Friday night before the party."

On the Friday night in question, Klarissa and Hektor took a little flat wagon with them. It was the one they made out of old crates, using the cushioned wheels from a retired baby buggy. The cart was contrived during the war. The boys used it to transport two large milk cans filled with water from the closest hydrant to their grandparents.

"It's a good thing we didn't dispose of that contraption. Looks like it's coming in handy once again," said Hektor's father.

Shortly after dark, they took off for Bredeney. It was a good hour of walking and pulling the empty wagon. Coming back with the loaded cart and maneuvering the sidewalks in the dark took them better than two hours to reach Kupferstrasse. Much to everyone's relief, none of the bottles broke, and no one paid any attention to the "smugglers." They might have been in trouble if the wrong people discovered their contraband.

Helena did a lot of baking during the week before the event. One of her specialties was cheesecake. She wanted to bake it on Saturday night. Everyone had taken their baths and gone to bed. She had to wait to take the cake out of the oven.

Hektor got up at eleven o'clock to use the loo. When he saw lights on in the kitchen, he thought perhaps someone forgot to turn them off. As he quietly pushed open the door adjacent to the kitchen, he had the shock of his life.

Here was his mother in full view. She was stark naked except for a half-apron tied around her waist. She was standing bent over with her pendulous breasts swinging in midair. She held the oven door with her left hand and a toothpick in her right to inspect the cheese-cake for readiness to come out of the oven.

Hektor was glad that his mother was so absorbed by her task; she never knew she had an audience. He thought he had seen it all! He tiptoed back to his bed, pinching himself all the way and hoping he would not burst out laughing. Getting safely back to his room, he hid under the featherbed and dissolved in laughter.

Finally, the day had arrived. The Birkens were dressed in their very best clothes, most of which were tired looking and worn. At least everything was clean and mended. Albert's suit, of course, was the exception. He was one of the few boys who had a new suit in an appropriate color and style for the affair. Once the congregation was seated, the makeshift bell at the makeshift church was rung, and the music produced on the out-of-tune piano accompanied the proces-sional. The confirmands were marching in pairs, the boys followed by the girls.

Once everyone was seated, Pastor Tranig called up the confirmation class members one at a time to the provisional altar. He would lay his left hand on their heads while reading their respective confirmation verses from the certificate he was holding with his right.

"Look at him. He has a tough time reading those certificates. Guess he didn't memorize our confirmation verses. Bastard!" said one of the boys. Most of the kids could hear what was said.

At last the boring sermon and the endlessly dragged-out affair concluded. Frau Tranig, who acted as the temporary organist, pounded out the recessional. The music was so bad Hektor wanted to cover his ears. There was the shaking of hands along with the best wishes.

"Of course Frau Pastor Tranig and I will be most delighted to join you for dinner this afternoon." The old buzzard knew where the victuals would be exceptional.

The dining room table was fully opened, and a second large table was set in the living room. Chairs were borrowed from friends and family. There were more than thirty people at the feast. All but Hektor were enjoying the beer garnered from the English officers' canteen. In addition, Grandpa Krämer was serving some of his homemade wine. By the time the main course was set before the guests, most of them were in a celebratory mood despite the pastoral presence.

As nothing was squandered in those days, Helena opted to prepare only half the calf for Albert's confirmation. She couldn't be sure what would be available by the time it was Hektor's turn. The meat was preserved. It might not be as good as fresh; nevertheless, having the certainty of veal for the event was reassuring. If something better came along, the canned meat would never go to waste.

For Albert's confirmation feast, the veal had been roasted to perfection. Helena was known for her wonderful mashed potatoes. They had white asparagus, albeit canned. It was too early in the season for fresh. Her Hollandaise sauce was masterful. Everyone needed a brandy to help with the digestion of the rich meal; their systems were no longer used to such calorie-laden morsels.

Late in the afternoon, Helena's Kaffeeklatsch was another major success. As her helpers carried in the numerous tortes and cakes, Hektor smiled to himself when the cheesecake was presented with great pride. Of course, no one was aware of the sideshow to which he had been privy the night before. He was still seeing those pendulous breasts swinging in front of his eyes.

The tables were reset, using her *Königlich Tettau* dishes. She was so proud the service for twenty-four persons survived the war. Linens and napkins, embroidered by Helena and friends when she was a young woman, had been part of her dowry.

Her whole show went smoothly. If there were any problems with the celebration, they were minor.

"Who was so careless with my coffeepot? That's a shame it was damaged. I suppose I should be happy it was only a piece of the spout and not the whole pot. I'll need to consult with Anton at Michelle's. He might come up with a way of fixing the thing."

Later they outfitted the slightly damaged coffeepot with a white, soft plastic spout. It continued to be a conversation piece for years. Helena simply could not part company with her precious coffeepot.

The celebration came to a fitting conclusion when Albert and his mother participated in his first Holy Communion on Maundy Thursday. It was a tradition to which all Protestant churches held. Hektor and his father could observe the event; however, they were not allowed to take communion. Alex was still a Catholic, and Hektor was not confirmed yet. For now, he was pleased to have experienced the rehearsal for his own confirmation in two years.

Hektor's long summer vacation from school started on August third. Helena had no idea how she would keep her growing boy busy in things other than always having his nose in a book. Lately he couldn't wait for the arrival of the morning paper and read the daily chapter of Daphne du Maurier's *Rebecca*.

"Why don't you help me weave some new baskets?" posed his mother.

"You must be joking, Mother. That's women's work. Where did you get the cane, and where did you learn how to make baskets?"

"I cut these young canes from the willow tree that's been growing for years by the wall in the backyard. My favorite aunt, Aunt Mathilde, in Swabia taught me basket weaving when I was a young girl. Later I had more instructions at the Stiftsgrundhof. It wouldn't hurt you at all to learn something new and different to do with your hands."

"Learning to fashion wreaths and bouquets from Herr Fillipu-sis, our friendly neighborhood florist, is handy work enough for me. Peter Siebenschneider and I are looking forward to our gathering of greens and trim in the woods this fall. We'll open our own little stand at the cemetery and undersell the florists. Herr Fillipusis will be pissed by our competition."

"You can't do that to that kind old man!"

"And why not? He's the one who's taught me 'business is business.' I'll show him how good a teacher he's been."

Just then Peter stormed into the store. Hektor could tell right away that something terrible happened.

"You won't believe what I experienced this morning. Hildegard, some of the other kids, and I went to the Ruhr and got into the water. It felt great to swim in the cool waters in this hot weather we've been having. Hildegard tried to get her feet wet and lost her footing on the slippery rocks. She fell into the rushing river and drowned. None of us were aware she didn't know how to swim. Her funeral will be at the Ehrenfriedhof on Tuesday."

Helena listened to Peter, not wanting to interrupt his sad story. She knew that Hektor had never learned to swim and envisioned if it had been he instead of Hildegard. Fear struck into her heart, and she realized immediately that something needed to be done about it. Not having learned how to ride a bike was one thing; not knowing how to swim might mean death.

"I'm going to call Aunt Klara and see if you could spend a few weeks with her. I know they have that beautiful pool in Emmendingen—a perfect place for you to learn how to swim. The country air will do you good, and Aunt Klara will love having you visit."

Hektor couldn't believe what his mother was suggesting. Going on any kind of trip, and especially alone, was the furthest thing from his mind.

"Mutti, I will have to stay for Hildegard's funeral but will be more than happy to take you up on your offer to send me to Köndringen if Aunt Klara will have me.

"Let me call her right now."

The phone kept ringing while Helena shifted her weight from one foot to the other. "Darn, I should have gone to the loo before I dialed her number."

Just then she made out Klara's distinct voice on the other end of the line.

"Hallo, Klara, it's Helena calling. How are you? It's been a while since we spoke last."

"How nice to hear from you. I'm doing OK. I still miss my Rudi, but my French houseguests and the inn keep me busy. I've befriended a widower who moved here from the East. His name is Fritz, and he's become a big help to me. Don't get me wrong. He ain't sleeping with me, but he's good company and helpful. I'm thankful to have a man around the house. How are my boys, and how are you and Alex getting along?"

"The boys are doing fine, but they're growing up too fast. Albert is in the midst of his butcher apprenticeship, and Hektor is still enjoying his new teachers. I'm pleased to learn that you found Fritz and that he is helping you with all that is on your daily plate. How would you feel about Hektor coming to visit you for a few weeks during his vacation?"

"That would be wonderful. How soon could he be here?"

"I'll have him on the train in five days. A schoolmate of his drowned in the Ruhr today because she didn't know how to swim. It's just terrible. By any chance, might Hektor be able to get swimming lessons at the pool in Emmendingen?"

"I don't know about lessons, but my French guys are excellent swimmers and practically have been spending all day at the pool during the hot weather we've been having. I'm sure they'll just love teaching Hektor, and he might even learn some French in the process."

"That sounds great, Klara. You are a savior, and I know Hektor will love being with you. Thanks for coming to my rescue. The death of that girl scared me, knowing that Hektor never had a chance to learn how to swim. Good talking with you. We'll do it again soon. Unbeknownst greetings to Fritz. Bye for now."

"Goodbye, Helena. Thanks for allowing me to have Hektor for a few weeks."

Hildegard's tragic death and the funeral had a devastating effect on young and old in the neighborhood. Helena was pleased she arranged the trip south for Hektor. As planned, he was on the train to Köndringen on August 8.

Klara, François, and Gerard met Hektor at the station. He had been wondering how he could get his two suitcases to the Lion Inn. He hugged Aunt Klara and shook hands with the men after they introduced themselves. Hektor was wondering if these were the two single men Aunt Klara had mentioned earlier when Mother had retrieved her belongings the year before. They sure were friendly enough. Each took one of his suitcases without much ado, allowing him to walk with Aunt Klara and just converse with her. François and Gerard probably understood little of what was being said, especially by Aunt Klara, speaking in the thickest of Badenser dialects.

Arriving at the inn, Hektor made the acquaintance of Fritz and the two French couples. He had been right in his assumptions about François and Gerard, as he was soon to discover. Taking his suitcases to his former room, François tried to hug him just a little too tightly. Hektor didn't say anything but gently backed away from the man.

As it turned out, François and Gerard were the avid swimmers and would be his swimming instructors. They were off to the Emmendingen swimming pool the next day right after breakfast. The guys had requisitioned Uncle Rudi's motorcycle with a sidecar as soon as they had spotted it upon their arrival. Klara didn't mind, since they took good care of it. It had been sitting unused in the workshop all through the war. François drove, and Gerard sat behind him on the seat, hugging him firmly. Hektor and all their stuff rode in the sidecar.

The first challenge came in the shower and change room. Speaking nothing but French, the two men attended each other in the process of undressing and soaping each other while they encouraged Hektor to be an active participant. François was clearly the more aggressive of the two; he actually touched Hektor where he didn't want to be touched. For him it was déjà vu. Hektor scrambled away and quickly got into the new swimsuit his mother had purchased before leaving for the journey.

They were off to the first swimming lesson. The guys slowed down their rapid French and made every effort to convey through gestures and facial expressions what they were trying to teach Hektor. Within a week, Hektor felt confident enough to venture into the deep end of the pool without any trepidation. Although François and Gerard tried on numerous occasions to encourage him to enjoy a ménage à trois, he succeeded in declining their invitations without hurting anyone's feelings.

By the time he returned to his family a month later, Hektor had savored a most enjoyable reunion with Aunt Klara, loved making Fritz's acquaintance, and took pride at having become comfortable with swimming. Saying his goodbyes, he was startled when François and Gerard kissed him deeply on the mouth, much to Aunt Klara's and Fritz's chagrin. Hektor just shrugged and muttered, "Must be the French way of saying *au revoir*."

Chapter 17

Two years at the Wackenburgschule had gone by all too quickly. Hektor couldn't wait for summer vacation to come to an end; he was anxious for his classes with Herr Krantopf to resume. To his horror, he learned his old neighborhood school on Kupferstrasse would reopen in late August 1947.

He and other children in the neighborhood needed to switch back to their former school. Hektor pleaded with his teacher to intercede on his behalf and to keep him at the Wackenburgschule.

"I don't mind the long walk to school; I got used to it. It often gave me time to think about what I learned on a given day. I don't want to become acquainted with new teachers. I am perfectly happy with the teacher I have now!" Mother Birken got into the act.

"Stop making such a fuss about going back to your old school. You are thirteen years old. Grow up! This is the real world. You might as well get used to German bureaucracy. I'm sure there will be teachers at Kupferschule you will learn to like."

Hektor swallowed hard and learned his lesson. No matter how much he complained about the transfer being unfair, there was no way around it. He had to get used to new classmates and new teachers.

His classroom teacher was the principal of the Kupferschule, Herr Rektor Nagelmann. *How would he ever become used to that guy? He was so different from Herr Krantopf. Different, but not bad.*

Hektor's objections to transferring to Kupferschule were known by Rektor Nagelmann; Herr Krantopf made a special effort to meet with Hektor's new mentor. He made sure Rektor Nagelmann continued to build on the previous foundation. All this was unbeknownst to Hektor.

Obviously, Mr. Krantopf did not have the time to go around to various schools that were reopening and plead the case of each student who didn't want to transfer back to his former neighborhood school. Hektor realized quickly that Rektor Nagelmann was more like Mr. Krantopf than he was different; they practiced similar educational principles and fostered independent thinking and intellectual growth.

During the next two years, Hektor truly learned to appreciate Rektor Nagelmann. He felt confident that he would be steered in the proper direction relative to his educational concerns.

Chapter 18

HEKTOR was confirmed March 14, 1948. He had come full circle since experiencing Albert's confirmation celebrations. Albert had worn his dark suit only one time. By now he had outgrown it. Helena took a good look at Albert's well-rested suit and ran her hands caressingly over the fine fabric.

"This suit will do you just fine. It's still beautiful and like new; but of course, Tailor Wibbelschnitz will have to recast it to make it fit you. You are so much smaller than your brother, and you are right— you would never make it as a butcher. What a shame it would be to let the suit go to waste. Unless you grow a lot, you might be able to wear it to dancing school."

"I hope to God I won't have to wear the same suit five years from now. You can't seriously expect me to take after you in height; I like to think Dad passed on some of his genes when he fathered me."

"I have no idea who you take after; sometimes I wonder. You certainly are different from your brother. By the way, your grandfather asked me to pick out fabric for a dressy winter coat for you. We'll wait a couple of years to have Tailor Wibbelschnitz make it." That was OK with Hektor.

"I can wait. Since I'm marching down the aisle in my brother's hand-me-down, I won't be expected to grovel in thanks before Grandfather, or will I?"

"You certainly will have to express your thankfulness to your grandparents for the coat material. I don't understand why you dislike your grandfather. I just don't."

"I'll tell you why! For as long as I can remember, I always felt just tolerated by him. And guess what? For some time now, I have done everything to express my reciprocation of that feeling. I simply don't like him for wanting to impose his ideas and wishes on my life. I am who and what I am!" He better learn that about me." He hoped his mother got his message.

Everything was the same, including the boring afternoons with Pastor Tranig; the tedious test and lousy questions; and the identical production. The sole difference was Hektor's confirmation verse. The meal and Kaffeeklatsch were carbon copies of Albert's. Fortunately for Helena, there was no repeat of the special attraction on Saturday night. Hektor had wondered how he might react to those pendulous breasts at this point in time?

Normally, parents gave their children a piece of jewelry, specifically a watch, on the occasion of their confirmation. In postwar Germany, that wasn't possible.

In spring 1948, Hektor's father needed to take his pocket watch to a jeweler for cleaning and repair. It was the famous egg-shaped pocket watch that Grandpa Birken had purchased at the World's Fair in Saint Louis in 1904.

The watch could be set to chime and thus act as an alarm clock. Hektor never knew his paternal grandparents. Grandpa Birken apparently liked to get away from everything and would occupy his box at the Apollo Theater across the street from the hotel in Düsseldorf. When it was time for him to rise from his daily nap, his trusted American chimer would waken him.

Before Hektor's father took the heirloom watch for repair, he detached its heavy, eighteen-karat gold fob and kept it safe. When he went to retrieve the watch a few weeks later, the shopkeeper regretfully informed Alex that there was a break-in at the store. One of the items missing was the treasured pocket watch. Alex was convinced the watch had caught the repairman's eye.

Hektor often wondered what his paternal grandparents might have been like. *Would they have been as loving as his father and his sister, Aunt Marianne?* From the few photographs he had seen of his long-dead grandparents, they appeared to be such different people. He was sad to realize that he would never know them. Although indirectly, genes of his unknown grandfather would eventually be part of his persona, as he, too, would become a wanderer on the earth.

As Hektor's confirmation moved closer, the family was discussing the possibility of using the gold fob of the lost watch and fashion it into three insignia rings for Alex and his two sons. Naturally, it was just a discussion. Hektor would have preferred a watch. That was still out of the question. None were to be had at that moment in time. The ring was a suitable substitute.

"But was he really getting it?" He kept plaguing his mother again and again.

The day after the test, Hektor continued hounding Helena with his questions. She broke down.

"You are the most impatient person I have ever known. Patience is a virtue, but certainly not one of yours. When they passed that out, you were absent. Yes, we had the rings made. Here is yours. Try it on and make sure it fits."

"Mutti, it's beautiful. I like the oval shape and the way the jeweler wove my four initials together. To me, it's a real connection to the grandfather I never knew. Thank you, thank you!"

"Well, I'm glad you like it. Just don't tell your brother; he is to receive his at the time you will have yours given to you. Are you happy now?"

"Yes! At least one thing will make this confirmation different from my brother's. It's too bad I have to take it off. I can't wait to wear it!" He was smiling as he headed for his room; he was so tired of always having played second fiddle.

Chapter 19

CHRISTMAS 1948 was very special to most German families living in the western part of the country. It was the first Christmas since the Reichsmark had been devalued ten to one on June 20. Soon the Deutschmark came into circulation. Miraculously, everything that could only be had on the black market became available in abundance.

The heart of the city was the center of attraction for many families. Window-shopping was the thing to do during the weeks before the feast. Storefronts and windows were bursting with merchandise of the finest quality, tempting eager eyes and encouraging shoppers to fulfill their long-stifled desires for a new garment or even a piece of jewelry. Anything was now available that had been denied most Germans during the years of war and the deprivation of the postwar era.

Helena and Alex Birken were no different. They had taken their two sons part of the way by streetcar into town. The tracks of streetcar number eighteen were mostly working; they had to walk the last three minutes toward the Hauptbahnhof. Alex, still using two canes, had reluctantly come along. Albert, going on seventeen, had grudgingly joined the shopping spree. Hektor, almost fifteen, could not wait to see the wonders of the mercantile world. There were so many things he wanted.

They stood in front of the Deiter's jewelry store and admired a plethora of watches in every shape, size, and price.

"If I could ask for only one thing, I would love to have my own watch," said Hektor. "I'm so tired of always having to approach total strangers on the street and having to ask, 'What time is it?' When I start taking the train to Steele next year while I attend the School of Commerce, it sure would be nice to have my own watch." Helena looked at her younger son.

"Of course a gold watch is out of the question. Which of these *Kienzle* watches do you like? They are an excellent make; the company has been in the watchmaking business since 1883. These are made of stainless steel; they are durable and quite attractive."

"I like that rectangular one with the light-brown leather strap. It is different."

"That's a pretty hefty price. Let me talk it over with your father when we get home tonight. There are many other things you will need. You have to have new shoes, socks, underwear, pajamas, and some decent dress shirts and pants. You know we weren't able to buy anything for years. The watch is very nice but perhaps more costly than we can afford this year." Hektor's penchant for window-shopping quickly dissipated. His mother studied his face.

"Don't look so disappointed. You can't always get what you want. You are not a baby any longer. Be a little more mature about this. I can't just think of your needs. The rest of us came through the war as well."

She hadn't done it in years. She was ready to slap his face. Helena could tell her last comments clearly put a damper on the situation. For now, she chose not to pursue the issue any further. She had to think of Albert and others in the family—and, of course, she had to be practical. Helena was never given to flights of extravagance. She was anything but a spendthrift; some would describe her as a dyed-in-the-wool pragmatist.

A year later Hektor was to discover how others lived. Greta

Beerenbaum would not have batted an eye; she would have bought the watch on the spot. A couple hundred marks were a drop in the bucket in Greta's budget, if there even existed such a thing. But this was Christmas 1948. There would be many changes in Hektor's life in the new year. He had no idea what lay beyond.

Hektor occasionally helped in the butcher shop to earn some pocket money. The enterprise had undergone numerous transformations. Before and during the war, it changed from a butcher shop to a grocery store; right after the war, it was converted into a fish market. Now that Alex was back on board, more or less, and Albert was aspiring to join the long line of master butchers in the family, the time had come to return to their traditional trade.

Mortar and bricks in the three store windows were replaced with plate glass, one of the first investments to remove the last vestiges of the war years. Now fresh meats, other products, and sausages could be displayed enticingly for the eager customers.

"I'll handle regular meats and sausages. Just don't ask me to touch things like liver, tongue, or tripe. The thought of handling that stuff could make me heave." With those disclaimers announced, Hektor enjoyed decorating the windows or operating one of the cash registers.

Hektor went into the city on the second Sunday of Advent. The stores were open from one to five o'clock on the three Sundays before Christmas. At Wetzels, he bought beautiful silk ties for his father and brother; for his mother, he selected a silk square. The dominant color was lavender—her favorite. Hektor loved the rich feel of genuine silk in his hands. He was pleased with his purchases. Needless to say, there wasn't enough money in his wallet to even think about buying presents for other relatives.

The family business closed at noon on Christmas Eve. The last customers had turned their backs toward Helena after she had dispensed cooking instructions for a particular roast, punctuated by a *Frohe Weihnachten!* [Merry Christmas!] as they exited the Birken

Butchery. Store and household help made sure the business and home were spotless. They were given their Christmas presents and sent on their merry way.

Alex, as usual, was the first to take his bath. He had last-minute chores in the family parlor. Of course, the days of utter secrecy had passed. Albert and Hektor no longer believed the Christ Child to be the bearer of the generous Christmas bounty. Nevertheless, Alex's jobs were to decorate the tree and to display the presents in designated spots. Helena arranged the Rosenthal bowl in the center of the buffet; it was filled with home-baked cookies, marzipan, and wonderful chocolates. Hektor's spot was to the left and Albert's to the right of the centerpiece. They had their own plates of goodies, always to be replenished from their mother's precious china bowl when no one was looking.

Helena's entry into the dining room was the signal to fetch the elderly neighbor couple from upstairs; the traditional Christmas Eve meal of *Hasenpfeffer and Spätzle* was about to be served. For the first time in many years, glasses of brilliant red wine were lifted in celebration of the good times having come upon them.

The idle chitchat seemed to go on forever. Hektor was dying to see what fabulous presents his parents selected for him. Actually, he kept envisioning the watch he so admired a few weeks ago. He was certain Mom convinced Dad it was a suitable gift for him since he told her he could care less about any of the other stuff. Obviously, he could use all of those other things but would be happiest if he just got the watch. Helena could tell by Hektor's demeanor he was anxious to move into the parlor.

"Shall we wait to have the *Schwarzwälder Kirschtorte* until after the presentation of the gifts?" she intoned.

Hektor nodded affirmatively; Albert just plain didn't care. He had a pretty good idea what would be there for him—mostly new uniforms and sturdy, sparkling white butcher aprons. Albert was eager to get out of the house. Much to his parents' chagrin, he was more interested in being with his girlfriend, Margarethe, and her family.

Helena rose from her comfortable chair and headed for the parlor door while making an inviting gesture to the others. She sat down at the piano and played *Ihr Kinderlein kommet* [Come little children, come ...], the familiar cue that all was in readiness.

"Thank God we don't have to recite one of those darn lengthy Christmas poems any longer," he whispered to Albert. That would have held up the production for another fifteen minutes.

He caught a glimpse of the beautiful tree standing as always in the corner to the left of the parlor door. His father had hung all the glass ornaments and electric candles that survived the war. The finishing touches were the perfectly draped icicles at the tip of each and every branch giving the tree a silvery mantle that was unique; there were no carelessly tossed strands of tinsel on this tree. Hektor headed straight for the left side of the buffet.

He spotted immediately a cap, a woolen scarf, and mittens his mother had knitted lovingly during many nights in the past few months. There were three beautiful dress shirts, socks, some much-needed new underwear, a pair of pajamas, and several other things. *Where the hell is my watch?* he thought. *It should have been prominently displayed. Guess they opted after all not to buy it for me!*

He gave all of his wonderful presents merely a fleeting glance. He looked first at his mother and then at his father and managed an insincere smile along with, "Thank you for the lovely presents. They are all things I can use." As he caught Albert's eye, his brother managed to shrug, wanting to convey he didn't know what was going on.

Before Hektor found a chair and sat down, he grabbed a piece of the marzipan from the large Rosenthal bowl.

"Why do you look so unhappy? Didn't the presents we selected give you any joy whatsoever?" his mother asked softly. "We thought you would appreciate these items you truly need. I know what you are looking for, but it shouldn't be the only thing to make you enjoy this special Christmas. Why don't you look at your gifts more carefully? Perhaps the Christ Child's messenger was a bit devious."

He got off his duff and walked over to the buffet to take a second look at his other gifts. First he squeezed the socks, the scarf, and the knitted mittens. He peeked inside the collars of the shirts and fingered the underwear. Finally, he took a closer look at the new pajamas. He noticed the pocket on the left side of the fancy pajamas was slightly bulging. Upon closer inspection, Hektor discovered the slender black box stuck in the breast pocket. He popped it open with a big grin on his face. The Kienzle watch was staring back at him. His parents had bought it after all.

Hektor walked over to his parents and gave them hugs. The expression of his appreciation in this manner had become a rarity in recent years—hugging, especially his father, no longer seemed appropriate. However, on this occasion, it was the only way for him to show the joy he was experiencing.

He made sure the watch was wound and set at the correct time. As he put it on, he determined he would never take it off, except when taking his weekly bath.

"With the fluorescent dial, I'll be able to tell time even in the darkness of night. What a wonderful thing! I'll never again have to bother others to learn the time of day!"

In the course of time, he purchased or was given all sorts of watches. Some would be far more valuable than the stainless steel Kienzle he received from his parents on Christmas Eve 1948. Sadly, he lost it while skiing for the first time in Oberstdorf in 1953. Apparently, the leather strap broke and the treasured object was lost in the fluff of abundant snow. He liked other watches he acquired in his lifetime, but somehow he remained partial to the old Kienzle. True, it was just an object, but he felt like he had lost an old friend.

Many years later Hektor would reflect on the happenings during the Christmas holidays of 1948. The concept of and the telling of time had taken on a difference in importance. Laura had introduced him to an old English prayer whose author remains unknown. Hektor chose to live by its tenets for the years to come:

Take time to work, it is the price of success.
Take time to think, it is the source of power.
Take time to play, it is the secret of perpetual youth.
Take time to read, it is the foundation of wisdom.
Take time to be friendly, it is the road to happiness.
Take time to dream, it is hitching your wagon to a star.
Take time to love and be loved, it is the privilege of the gods.
Take time to look around, it is too short a day to be selfish.
Take time to laugh, it is the music of the soul.

The Birken Saga
Book 2

A Wanderer on the Earth

1948–1952

Chapter 1

AT the end of the school year, Hektor scheduled a conference with Rektor Nagelmann, his principal and teacher at the Kupferschule. The outcome would ultimately shape the rest of Hektor's life. His mentor looked forward to the meeting since he was very much interested in helping Hektor find answers to the many questions concerning the boy's education.

"What do you intend to do with your life? Where do you see yourself going when you leave this school a year down the road? You have excellent skills in English and have mastered our German language far beyond your age."

Hektor had known these questions would be asked of him one of these days. A decision had to be made of how to proceed with his education. And so he blurted it out.

"What I really would like to do when I finish here is to attend the *Folkwangschule* and study acting." Rektor Nagelmann peered over his wire-rimmed glasses and was all ears. He seemed totally surprised, his face spelling all sorts of questions.

"Have you discussed this with your family?"

"No, I haven't! I'm sure they'll be shocked to learn of my intentions, and I am positive there will be a lot of opposition."

Hektor had made up his mind to confront his family at the next opportunity. His parents had invited Hektor's grandparents for Sunday dinner. He walked into the family dining room. At the head of the table sat his grandfather dominating the conversation. Reflections from the chandelier bounced off the bald head of the old man. His strange-looking eyeglasses clasped the bridge of his bulbous nose and appeared to be slipping off the dominant facial appendage. Grandfather's beady eyes were fixed on his fourteen-year-old grandson. Hektor needed to pinch himself not to laugh at the sight of the fat jowls drooping off the much-feared man's face. When his grandfather finally spoke, Hektor knew he was in for a confrontation with his nemesis.

"Your brother is doing well in the second year of his apprenticeship. I hear nothing but praise from his master butcher. Do I dare ask what trade you would like to learn?"

"I don't wish to be apprenticed in any trade; my visions for my life are very different from yours. After my next school year, I am entering the *Folkwangschule* to study acting." Hektor didn't blink an eye glaring at his grandfather. His stance conveyed what the expected reaction would be. Grandfather cupped his ear.

"Did I understand you correctly? Did you say acting?" He picked up his stein and took a healthy swig from the vessel. It was obvious he wanted to wash the bad taste from his mouth. Hektor nearly burst out laughing contemplating his grandfather's foam-covered mustache, almost Hitleresque in shape. The old man stared at Hektor and his father.

"You must be joking!" His eyes bulged as he slammed the *Bier Stein* on the highly polished surface. Beer was spilled all over. Hektor's mother covered her mouth as she beheld the ugly scar left on the precious dining room table that survived the war without a scratch. Hektor looked his grandfather straight in the eyes.

"As a matter of fact, joking is the furthest thing from my mind. I've never been more serious about anything!"

"Who the hell do you think you are talking to?"

"Sorry to disappoint you and to be disrespectful, Grandfather, but you are the one who set the tone for this discussion. I may and I may not become an actor, but one damn thing is for sure: I shall never be a butcher. There are already enough in this family!" Hektor stayed out of striking distance, knowing the old geezer might have struck him with one of his crutches. He realized his fate was sealed.

"There will be no dilettantes in this family." Grandpa Krämer glared at Hektor and faced his son-in-law as he struck the dining room table repeatedly with his balled fist.

"Alex, I want you to remove this boy immediately from that school where such crazy ideas seem to be hatched and planted in his head. You apprentice him posthaste in a respectable trade. No grandson of mine will ever stand on any stage making an ass of himself." He reached for the crutches and pushed himself out of his chair; his arthritic hips were giving him fits.

"When I come back from taking a piss, I expect to hear an acceptable answer to my demands."

Stumbling back onto the scene, Grandpa caught everyone looking at him in shock. His pants were still unzipped; he had obviously pissed all over himself and soiled his pants to boot. Hektor's mother walked over to her aging father and guided him back to the bathroom. Embarrassed, Grandma and Helena undressed and cleaned the old man. One of Alex's robes would have to do the trick. He was still fuming at Hektor when he finally emerged from the WC.

"This is all your fault; it was your crazy scheme that caused me to have the accident. If I could stand alone on my two feet, I would horsewhip your ass like I used to do years ago, you bastard."

"I always knew you enjoyed whipping us. I hate saying it, but it doesn't bother me seeing you humiliated. You seem to thrive on doing it to others and especially me. What just happened to you is exactly what you deserved—and I should feel sorry for you?"

"How dare you speak to your grandfather that way!" screamed his mother.

"And why not? He threatened me and called me a bastard. Last I knew, it was Dad who fathered me and not the milkman." Hektor wanted to walk out of the room, but his father grabbed his arm and stopped him.

"You better forget about this acting idea. Who do you think would pay for you to attend the *Folkwangschule?*

"Frankly, I thought you and Mom would since my entire education was screwed up by the damn war. Because of lacking more than two years of schooling, I can't even consider enrollment at a *Gymnasium* [preparatory high school]. I'm just sick of running into roadblocks everywhere." His father understood Hektor's dilemma.

"When you were a little boy, you used to say you wanted to become a pastry chef. Maybe I should speak to Herr Nudelmann at his bakery. Becoming a baker might be an honorable and acceptable trade for you to learn. It might appease your grandfather."

"Why do I need to appease him? It's my life we are talking about. Personally, I don't give a damn what he thinks of me!" Hektor had to have the last word in this argument.

His father and Herr Nudelmann executed the contract. Hektor began his three-year apprenticeship during the next week. The following Sunday, sitting in his piss-soaked chair, the old man grinned with pleasure when Hektor was forced to tell him what had transpired.

"As you wished, my father took me out of school and enslaved me to this lousy bakery apprenticeship. I hope you are happy now that you have once again imposed your will on me. But let me assure you, the last word hasn't been spoken on this matter."

"Where did you learn to speak in that way? Count your blessings that I'm handicapped. If I could, I'd give you the whipping of your life!"

Hektor was tempted to spit into the old man's face, but he opted to just walk out of the room and sought his grandmother in the kitchen. He liked having one of her cookies, but he found little else to talk about. His grandmother knew how hurt he was by his grandfather's bullheadedness. Hektor was glad when he could escape.

)(

He didn't know where he got the gumption, but on the Saturday concluding the sixth and final week of his probationary period, he stepped into Baker Nudelmann's office. The desk was covered with all sorts of papers slightly dusted with flour.

"Sir, I won't be back on Monday. I've hated every second of being under your roof. This isn't the life I've envisioned for myself. It's my grandfather who forced my father's hand to apprentice me to you. It's not what I want. I realize my educational dreams were destroyed by the war, but I will not be sacrificed on the altar of tradition. I will never be a baker, a tradesman, or anything that would please my mother's father. I hate the man and am convinced he has had no use for me from the day I was born."

Herr Nudelmann sat behind his desk, his mouth agape. Hektor thought he might have given the man a heart attack.

"Are you OK, Herr Nudelmann? I didn't mean to shock you!"

"That you did! But I'm OK. I'm glad you spoke up and regret that you feel the way you do about your grandfather. That said, I wouldn't want someone working for me for three years, hating every moment. More power to you; you'll do OK in life." He got out of his chair and reached for Hektor's contract in the safe. Tearing it to pieces, he handed it to the astounded boy.

"You'll catch hell from your folks, but I'm proud of you for speaking up." He shook Hektor's hand and wished him well. Hektor couldn't wait to get home and have dinner with his family. When the last person around the table was finished eating, he felt emboldened enough to share his news with the family.

"I'm going back to school on Monday. I'm all done with my trials at the bakery." He threw the torn contract on the table.

"Herr Nudelmann was happy to let me out of it when I told him that I was forced into slave labor and that I didn't want any part of it. I told him that it was Grandpa's wish and not mine to become a baker."

The expected pandemonium broke out. He was prepared for Papa Alex's choleric outbursts, but in the end, Hektor returned to school for one more year. When his grandfather learned the following weekend what Hektor had done, he was furious with him for opposing his wishes.

"How dare you back out of a contract your father signed. What will people say about our honorable name?"

"Frankly, Grandfather, I don't give a rip!" He was tempted to use a gesture but decided he had done enough to convey to the old man that he was standing his ground.

While Hektor started to work at the bakery, his classmates were in recess. They had just started their final year at the *Volksschule* [basic school]. No one was more shocked to see Hektor grace the frame of the classroom door than Rektor Nagelmann. There was a frown of uncertainty on his face; he didn't trust his eyes.

"What are you doing here? Why aren't you at work at the bakery?"

"I hate to surprise you. I'm done with that episode in my life and am here to stay! Don't look so astounded! If you remember, I told you I wouldn't let myself be railroaded into a world I couldn't face for the rest of my life." Right after class, he cornered Rektor Nagelmann, who was eager to get back to his office.

"When may I have an appointment with you to discuss my immediate future?"

"How about tomorrow afternoon at four? My calendar is clear, and we can chat as long as you wish."

"Great! I have a thousand questions."

Arriving at his mentor's office the next afternoon, he was put at ease by the teacher who had become more than an educator to him—he became his ally and friend.

"Well, young man, what's on your mind today?"

"I know I can stay here for another year, but I want you to show me the way beyond this school year. Since an acting career seems to be clearly out of the question, I would like to pursue a teaching career. A classroom could become my stage."

"Are you suggesting that I am acting in class?"

"No and yes; you seem to enjoy dramatizing the points you are trying to make. You are not a buffoon, but you have a way of acting things out that make learning fun. I could see myself doing that in front of a class. Becoming a teacher would certainly be more acceptable to the whole clan than being on stage."

"Now that you're putting it this way, I have to agree with you. I do enjoy being in front of the class; however, I hate to put a damper on your aspirations. It will be next to impossible for you to pursue that educational track at this time. To follow an academic career, you should have been enrolled at a *Hochschule* at age ten. That couldn't be done because of the war."

"Why couldn't I go to a *Hochschule* now?"

"Hektor, no pedagogue in his right mind would put a fourteen-year-old in a classroom with ten-year-old children. You are a young man with developed ideas. Psychologically, you have a different mind-set than a child aged ten. It just won't be done.

"However, I am not an autocrat. I will set up appointments for you with a couple of high school principals. Knowing your interests, I am inclined to get in touch with the rectors at two *Humanistic Gymnasiums*. Don't be too disappointed when they reiterate what I have tried to explain to you."

At the first school, Hektor did not even get past the rector's secretary. When asking Hektor why he was there, she simply opened the door to her boss's office and whispered the reason for his appointment. The man raised his eyebrows and yelled loud enough for Hektor to hear what he had to say.

"I am too busy to waste my time on such a nonsensical idea. Tell him to learn a trade. Not everyone is fit for higher education!" Hektor was out of the office so fast he didn't know what hit him. He couldn't say that Rektor Nagelmann hadn't warned him.

The second contact was somewhat more positive. While the same negative explanation was put to him with reference to starting way back with ten-year-olds, Hektor was let down more gently. Rather than aiming to obtain his *Abitur* [equivalent to an Associate's degree], the suggestion was he apply to the *Handelsschule* [School of Commerce] and pursue a degree and career in business. At first that seemed like a cop-out. However, when he related the suggestion to his trusted mentor, the reaction was positive and his comments encouraging as well as guarded.

"You realize there will be an entrance exam. They are highly selective in terms of their admissions, although I am not concerned about that. The other negative element is you will have to commute by train. The school in Essen was destroyed during the war and is now housed in an old cloister in Steele. Train travel will add to the cost of your schooling; and of course, your parents will have to pay tuition. It is not a free educational ride."

Hektor didn't jump to any conclusions; he mulled over the suggestions the rector at the *Gymnasium* and Herr Nagelmann made. Finally, he wanted to discuss the issue with his mother. Helena was definitely the better choice. She had a pretty good idea what Hektor was going through.

Her own educational aspirations fell victim to the aftermath of World War I. Her father was of the opinion women should never pursue advanced studies. Hektor could never understand why his mother venerated her father the way she did; he was a tyrant and always enjoyed imposing his will on others. Helena was deprived of postsecondary schooling by design. Hektor knew he had an ally in his mother.

"How would you feel about sending me to the Handelsschule in Steele for two years?" His mother was perplexed.

"How will you get there? By train from Essen-West and changing trains at the Hauptbahnhof? Do you realize how long a day this will be for you? Classes will start at eight o'clock in the morning, and you will be there until three or four o'clock in the afternoon. During the long winter months, you won't come home until well after dark. And then there will be studying in the evening. And how much is the tuition?" The pragmatist had finally spoken.

"Mother, by the time I start attending the Handelsschule, I will be fifteen years old. What's the big deal about taking a local train? You sent Albert and me halfway across the country in the middle of a war when we were nine and eleven. Didn't you think that was pretty gutsy? The first thing that will have to happen is passing the entrance exam. The tuition is another issue." That probably should have been the first of all questions raised with his parents and was the real clincher. Hektor knew that anything costing money might cause a major catastrophe in the Birken household.

"Let me discuss it with your father; I might be more persuasive in loosening his tight purse strings." When she broached the subject after the evening meal, Alex became thoughtful.

"Who knows, by the time 1949 rolls around, things will be

better. I expect our business to pick up and make a greater profit one of these days. Let's look at the future more positively. Hektor's educational aspirations were thwarted often enough. We should make every effort to support him." Hektor was dumbfounded. *Was he listening to his father?*

For a moment, he shed any inhibitions. He gave his dad a bear hug. No words were spoken; none were needed. At that moment, they fully understood each other.